CW01643196

TELEMARKSKIING

RDICA

HALVOR KLEPPEN

TELEMARKSKIING

NORWAY'S GIFT TO THE WORLD

DET NORSKE SAMLAGET
OSLO 1986

© 1986 Det Norske Samlaget
Translated by Margaret Saltveit
and Margaret Wold
Printed by Brepols S.A., Belgium 1986
Produced by Boksenteret as, Oslo 1986

ISBN 82-521-2854-8

Edited in collaboration with Fred Olsen & Co, Åsnes
Skifabrikk A/S and Skimuseet in Oslo.

CONTENTS

A.BLOCH
83

PREFACE

The main purpose of this book is to link the new trend in skiing – the Telemark way – to Telemark's skiing traditions in the last century. It is in many ways a close relationship, but in other ways a distant one – separated by the history of skiing that lies between past and present. Another of my aims is to get people out skiing in «virgin» country, away from the groomed slopes and tracks, out in the woods and up on the moors, skiing the way people used to ski for fun, and at work, more than a hundred years ago.

I alone am responsible for the book, but the process of getting it ready for publication has involved many other people. If Bente Dysthe had not persuaded me out on the slopes to try Telemark skiing a couple of years ago, this book would never have been written. I am also especially indebted to Stein Ø. Engell of the Norwegian Professional Ski Instructors Organization, Erik Enitch of Scandinavian Mountain Equipment, Tor Erik Haanes Larsen of the Joint Office for the Sport of Skiing, Kjell Åsnes of the Åsnes Ski Factory, and Steinar Opstad, Timex Skiathlom. They approach the subject from different angles, and have spent valuable time advising me about the manuscript as it took form.

Curator Karin Berg, director of the Holmenkollen Ski Museum, gave me free access to the Museum's valuable photo archives, and many of the photographs in the book come from there. I can, incidentally, warmly recommend a visit to the Ski Museum when you are in Oslo. Everyone who is interested in skiing will find something of appeal – especially cross-country skiing enthusiasts.

The Author

TELEMARK IN 1886

Fridtjof Nansen wrote:

IN 1986,

During the world première of the Timex Skiathlom in Vrådal, Telemark, Gjermund Eggen said, in connection with the Telemark Combination:

«Telemark is the rightful home of skiing. The people of Telemark are unquestionably our country's best skiers, and if they are the best in our country, I can doubtless say, without fear of exaggeration, that they are also the world's best. They have taught the townspeople a completely new way of skiing, and have thereby raised the art of skiing to the heights it has achieved in recent years. Telemark skiers truly deserve our respect and thanks.»

«This is the right way to go in for skiing – it's fun! There's cross-country, ski jumping and slalom, using the same type of skis as were used across the fields of Telemark more than a hundred years ago. There is far too much specialization and seriousness in the field of skiing today, but the fun on skis that we have seen the start of today, can once more persuade people to experience many different skiing activities on the same pair of skis.»

THE RENAISSANCE OF TELEMARK SKIING

Around 1980, a number of Norwegian ski enthusiasts noticed that a distinctive type of skiing, with strange roots in Norway, had sprung into existence in the USA. In ski centers and the jet set's alpine haunts, young daredevils were skiing in a way that Norwegians had only seen photos of in old books about skiing. On closer inspection it appeared that this was the new trend in American skiing: Telemark skiing, or just – Telemarking. The Norwegians soon found out that it was not just one group of skiing goofs doing this, but hundreds – thousands – of skiers spread across the whole continent, who had been infected with what the German ski magazine LANGLAUF called «the Telemark Virus». All the American ski magazines «CROSS-COUNTRY SKIER», «CROSS-COUNTRY SKI MAGAZINE», «OUTSIDE», «BACK-PACKER», «POWDER», and many others had leading articles and reports with colour photos. And when Norwegians also found a whole page in TIME MAGAZINE with the title «The hills are alive with the sound of Telemarking», they realized that something big was going on. This had also been the case at home in Norway since 1980. N.P.S., the Norwegian Professional Ski Instructors Organization, dusted off the old textbooks and started courses in the Telemark turn, and the Åsnes factory started production of Norwegian Telemark skis. In 1984 the first Telemark Cup competition was held, in co-operation with the Joint Office for the Ski Industry, and the Telemark style of skiing suddenly achieved undreamt-of possibilities. In the winter of 1986, production of Telemark skis accounted for 25 % of the total production of the Åsnes ski factory, and demand is much greater than production. When the shipowner Fred Olsen launched his SKIATHLOM idea in the fall of 1985, it turned out to be an important element in the development away from special skis for alpine and cross-country skiing, and it opened a new era for skiing with the same pair of skis in different types of terrain. The SKIATHLOM world première took place in the Vrådal ski centre, in Telemark. Vrådal is in the same county borough as Morgedal, the cradle of skiing, and it was from Morgedal that the first ski tracks from Telemark went out into the world and made skiing an international sport. So it is fitting that the Telemark ski tracks, strengthened by new impulses, once more go out into the world

from the same district. After the première in Vrådal in the winter of 1986, about 10,000 people took part in skiathlom competitions in the USA and in Norway.

In Sondre Norheim's time skis were used for all sorts of fun. Slalom was «invented» in Morgedal, and ski jumping and cross-country skiing over the moors was a common pastime for both girls and boys. At the Huseby race in 1869 they combined jumping and cross-country with a little slalom at the turns. Around 1900 rules were laid down for the combination cross-country/jumping, and in Central Europe the alpine combination that we are familiar with – slalom, grand slalom and downhill – was developed. The split between Nordic skiing and alpine skiing led to increased specialization, and children had to have special equipment

Like a township in Telemark, Crested Butte is situated in a valley in Colorado.

On the right
The last international ski name from Telemark is the World Cup alpinist, Atle Skårdal from Lunde. He had his great breakthrough in the winter of 1986, and here he is trying the Telemark style for the first time.

almost before they could walk. There was no place for Telemark skiing in this dichotomy, so it was only practised by a few crazy ski instructors when they showed off their skill to other people. Even in the mountains of Norway the new, narrow cross-country skis were preferred – even if they were unsuitable equipment, and in many situations quite simply dangerous.

TIMEX
skiathlon
112

Marius Eriksen was Stein Eriksen's father and was himself a competent skiier. Eriksen was from Skien in Telemark, but in Oslo he ran a sports shop. He is also well known for the ski-harnesses he developed.

It was five American ski instructors and mountain skiers who started digging into the history of Norwegian skiing and unearthed the Morgedal technique. Doug Buzzell, Craig Hall, Greg Dalbey, Jack Marcial and Rick Borcovec were at that time in Crested Butte, Colorado, and had read the book «COME SKI WITH ME» by Stein Eriksen. There they read about his father Marius and the Telemark turn, and this inspired them to try it out in open country. Borcovec, the director of the Nordic Adventure Ski School, has said about these first experiments that it was the need to get away from the ski lifts and out into open, virgin skiing country that made them start to experiment. In 1971 they tried touring skis with loose bindings, and soon found out that ordinary alpine techniques were unsuitable in deep powder snow and mixed terrain.

«The snowplow was difficult in deep powder snow, and the parallel turn too unstable on free-heeled bindings with flexible boots. So we based the «new» Telemark style on a photograph we had seen of Stein Eriksen's father demonstrating the Telemark turn. With this photograph as the starting point we went on our own.»

In connection with this, the American ski historian Art Burrows wrote:

«Little did these five know that taking up this skiing technique again would lead to a renaissance of Telemark skiing. Its growing popularity marks the end of an era of specialisation, and for many people the Telemark style is the best kind of skiing.»

MORGEDAL – THE CRADLE OF SKIING

Morgedal lies in the county borough of Kviteseid in Telemark. Today Morgedal is a rural community on Highway E 76 between Western and Eastern Norway. In the 19th century there was also a certain amount of traffic between Morgedal and the rural communities that lay higher up in the mountains of Tele mark. But above all, it is a community with steep hills, fertile soil and a lot of snow in the winter. From the lake in the bottom of the valley the farms climb up the hillsides, bathed in the late afternoon sun. All the conditions here were favourable for skiing. Sondre Norheim triggered it off, the Hemmestveit brothers and others followed up, and between them they created a milieu that other communities had never seen the likes of. Torjus Loupedalen has described Morgedal around 1850:

«The community houses roughly speaking 500 people, whom it has to feed and clothe, and provide work and leisure activities for. It cannot manage to feed them all; many must go out begging, and many others leave, especially from the communities in western Telemark and those towards the south of the country. They take their crafts with them – making shoes, harness, weaver's shuttles – or go into service. But the community can provide fun for them. There is dancing on the village green in the summer, skiing in the winter and the fiddle and dancing all year round. And here we have the key to it: the energy and go of the people in this community had to find release, expression, form – and they find it in skiing.»

Slalom

This skiing term comes from Morgedal in Telemark. Today the word slalåm – or slalom – (from sla: «smooth and slanting hill», and låm: «track») can be found in all languages that have words connected with skiing. In the big New Norwegian Dictionary from 1986 we find the definition: «skiing down a slope.» The first time the word slalom appeared in print was in 1879, and later it was used in the newspapers in connection with the skiing competition in Seljord in 1886, where there was also combined slalom and jumping. In the first slalom competitions times were not recorded, only their style was judged. Earlier on, young ski enthusiasts in the rural communities of Telemark had practi-

The township is visited by many tourists on their way between Eastern and Western Norway, and «The Cradle of Skiing» has developed since the last world war to be a popular tourist area in Telemark. It is in this township that a local museum has been built to commemorate the Antarctic explorer, Olav Bjaaland. Bjaaland was the last great skier from Morgedal Ski Club. He received the Holmenkollen medal in 1912 both for his participation in the trip to the Antarctic and for his rapid cross-country skiing and excellent jumps in Holmenkollen. The King's Cup which he won in 1902 is the last which went to Morgedal, and with Bjaaland ended a ski era.

sed slalom and other types of ski tracks in open country.

Mikkel Hemmestveit said many years later that slalom was the oldest form of skiing in Telemark. The usual form of slalom was practised in the open country, across the fields, over stone walls and hillocks, in and out between the thickets and underbrush. The other form was «the reckless track», down precipitous slopes and steep hillsides, in and out between the trees and round rocks at reckless speed. It was this type of slalom skiing that Sondre Norheim was to do so much of.

Around 1890 the pioneers took skiing to the Central European countries, and after the Huseby competition in 1890, one found slalom being practised in Austria and Switzerland. Sigmund Ruud wrote:

«On the first slalom courses the turns were marked individually with flags or ribbons. The skiers had to keep to the outside of these markers – though how far outside them was immaterial. It was this type of slalom, together with other types of skiing, spread to other countries around 1890. The first slalom competitions that were organized in the Alps followed the Norwegian pattern.»

The Telemark Style

Many of those who watched the New Year's Ski Jumping Competition from Garmisch-Partenkirchen on January 1st. 1986 must have smiled to themselves. Some of the competitors had a little stick or twig in their hands, just as they did in Telemark in the old days. This was probably a passing phase, but even so, it is the over 100-year-old tradition of ski jumping that is easiest to trace back to Telemark. The Telemark style, with its characteristic landing, has been a feature of ski jumping throughout these years, and it all started as a study of the style practised by skiers from Morgedal.

Sondre Norheim's new Telemark skis, together with his new bindings, gave the skier a safe, supple style that it had previously been impossible to achieve. This was the style that the skiers from Telemark impressed the capital, Christiania, with. At that time most people jumped with their legs drawn up under them – the «drawn-

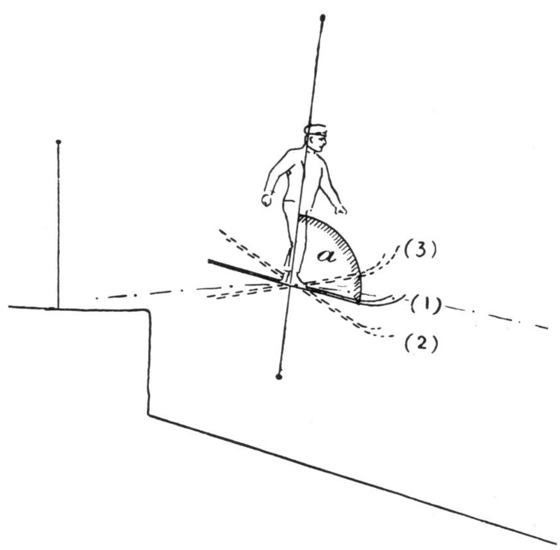

This illustration from Huitfelt in 1907 tells about the perfect Telemark style. (2) and (3) are obviously wrong. (1) shows the skis in a perfect angle.

«WE DO NOT CALL THEM SKIERS»

«The goal for our youth is to become all-round skiers mastering all the many finesses of skiing. Jumpers, can be created by people of the plains on a steel jumping hill on an American prairie. They even turn somersaults in the air instead of our simple-minded soaring. But we do not call them skiers; that is a more all-embracing and honourable term.»
(Amundsen)

Einar Landvik is considered by many people to be the top jumper in perfect Telemark style. Landvik is from Telemark and represented Rjukan Ski Club. After the Morgedal period ended, Einar Lundvik from Rjukan and Hans Kleppen from Bø were two of the skiers who kept up the Telemark reputation in international ski sport. Landvik was born in Kviteseid, but lived at Rjukan. He received the Holmenkollen Medal in 1925.

up style» – and on landing they bent one knee while keeping one ski in front of the other. Around 1880 the style of jumping changed, and the Telemark style in flight got its own norm, which required the jumper to stand erect, at full height, while leaning slightly forwards. He was allowed to make gentle movements with his arms to keep his balance. The skis were to be slanted carefully downwards towards the end of the jump, in order to come down parallel with the ground.

The Telemark Landing

Even today, ski jumpers have up to two points deducted from their total number of points for style if they do not execute the Telemark landing well enough. We find this bending of the knees in all types of skiing. When we ski down slopes that can present unforeseen obstacles or changing snow conditions, we have one ski slightly in front of the other. The knees act as shock absorbers, to tackle the unexpected obstacles. When the front ski is pushed out into a curve we have gone into the Telemark turn.

The Telemark Turn

The first tracks of the Telemark turn were made on the slopes of Morgedal. Whether Sondre Norheim was the first skier to practise it is an open question, but there is no doubt that it was his skiing equipment that made the execution of the turn into an art. Huge loads of hay were brought down from the moors in the winter, and it was useful to have a stem turn to control the sledges down the cart-tracks. They did not worry very much about braking – they took chances!

The Telemark turn was the best turn for

steering in deep powder snow, and when skiing enthusiasts in Colorado, in the USA, started using the turn again early in the 70's, it was because they wanted to find a steering turn for deep powder snow that could be used with free-heeled bindings. The fact that the Telemark turn developed into an art, with thousands of competitions on slalom slopes all over the world, says more about alpine skiers' need for something new, than anything else. They had taken ski lifts up and groomed slopes down all their skiing lives, and the longing for a change made them throw themselves over the Telemark turn.

If one tries to explain how the Telemark turn is executed, one finds a multitude of variants. Asbjørn Flemmen has written an excellent handbook, which is a good guide. We shall content ourselves with a simpler explanation of the essential features of the turn. Stein Øyvind Engell comes from Telemark, is a professional ski instructor, and

Above
The «drawn-up» style was not exactly attractive, but it was incredible how high the jumps were.

Below
From the «Telemarksvingen» by Asbjørn Flemmen we have taken this illustration of a Telemark turn. Flemmens book is full of good tips for those interested in learning the technique.

With this parallel swerve it was possible to either come to a stop on the outrun or to turn on an icy slope. Sondre Norheim was the first to demonstrate this turn in Kristiania. It got the misleading name, the «Kristiania turn», while the other turn which came from Morgedal (below), got the name the «Telemark turn».

in recent years he has been the foremost exponent of Telemark skiing:

«Find a gentle slope. Ski straight down the fall line. Move the ski that is to be the lower one forward, just enough for the tip of the inner ski to be a little in front of the binding of the outer ski, thus preventing the inner ski tip getting caught up in the binding of the front ski. There should also be some weight on the ski behind, so that it does not «flap». The knees are bent the Telemark way, and the arms held out to the side to achieve balance. Now move the front ski out in a gentle stem, then tilt it by bending the ankle and knee inwards. After you have got well into the turn, move the other ski inwards, so that the skis are parallel again.»

Stein Ø. Engell says that in deep snow it is important that there is more weight at the back, so that the front «stem ski» glides better over the snow. When the snow is deep, there is no stem sideslip, so one leans in a little to counteract the centrifugal force – how much, is determined by the speed. If the slope is very steep, the weight must be even further back, and the front stem ski must almost be steered crosswise to reduce speed.

The best way to learn the Telemark turn is on a course or at a ski school with professional ski instructors. After that it is just a question of practising and training as often as you can. The execution of a Telemark turn is not as easy as it looks, so, like other turns, it needs a bit of time spent on it.

The Christiania Turn

In 1901 three men were given the job of writing a set of rules for skiing. This set of rules most probably helped to ensure that many skiing expressions were not forgotten. Everybody knew of the Telemark turn, but when Sondre Norheim's parallel turn was called the Christiania turn in this set of rules, there were many who protested. Cato Aal, Kristian and Olaf Tandberg wrote the rules, and decided upon the name Christiania turn. Fritz Huitfeldt was furious, and said that this turn had nothing to do with Christiania. Later, they tried to correct this blunder in the rules by calling the two turns Telemark turn A and Telemark turn B, but by then the damage had already been done.

Many people will claim that this was a trifle, but if one reads foreign publications on skiing, one realizes that it is important that every detail is correct. The book «Total Telemarking» was published in the USA in 1984, and the author, Brad English, wrote there:

«To defeat their Telemark rivals, the Christianians Torjus and Mikkel Hemmestveit developed their own system of skidded, wide, parallel turns known today as «stem-christiania» or «christie-swing».

Just imagine! The Hemmestveit brothers were of course from Morgedal – not Christiania. They executed this turn and the Telemark turn the way they had learnt it at home in Morgedal from Sondre Norheim. With this technique they had won competitions in, of all places, Christiania, after Sondre had retired from competitive skiing. So one can safely say that the Telemark style, the Telmark turn and the Christiania turn are based on the tenant farmer Sondre Norheim's style of skiing.

SONDRE NORHEIM

The Father of Modern Skiing

«In Sondre the love of skiing is a quiet, glowing flame that burns brightly throughout his life. We see him gambolling up on the slopes, a ragged, happy little nipper; we see him old, poor and cold, waiting up among the trees until they call out – come on! And we see him wobbling down the steep hills – tired, grey, exhausted. But we also see the youngsters coming to fetch him, despite his age. He gives them his most precious possession – skiing.»

It was this man from Morgedal in Telemark, a poor tenant farmer and maker of weaver's shuttles who gave posterity a new sport. In the depths of the Norwegian winter, it gave them new opportunities for leisure activities and for exciting competitions. Torjus Loupedalen, who has written an interesting, colourful book about skiing in Morgedal, has given posterity an extraordinary insight into the start of modern skiing, from Sondre's childhood to old age – when he was still out on the slopes with the kids, a source of enormous inspiration and joy.

Sondre revolutionized skiing in many ways. He made the first experiments with ski equipment that we still use today. He was the first to use heel bindings, so that his skis stayed in place when he skied at his most reckless pace. He was the first to use waisted skis, so that it was easier to turn with them round trees and on steep slopes or at the bottom of the ski jump. A remarkable skier in every way, he was also the first person to make jumping and slalom into something more than just an aimless activity.

His exploits on skis became an art that we imitate even today. It was Sondre who, with the help of his new equipment, placed the steering ski in front of the other one in deep powder snow, so that unexpected hillocks or drops were easier to ski over. With bent knees, and always ready to face new obstacles with new techniques, he introduced a completely new way of skiing that could be practised in all sorts of terrain – Telemark skiing. The method he practised was so ingenious that we have today gone back to its origins in Morgedal and are witnessing a rebirth of the type of cross-country skiing that was based on the ideas of Sondre. We go skiing on modern skis with steel edges – and waisting that we owe to Sondre.

Sondre Norheim was born on the little

The small tenant farm, Øverbø in Morgedal where Sondre Norheim (left) was born in the summer of 1825. Here the Olympic flame was lit for the Olympic Games in Oslo, 1952, and in Squaw Valley in 1960 (see p. 60).

tenant farm of Øverbø, in Morgedal, on June 10, 1825. It was part of the Kleiv farm, and is still there, at the northernmost end of the community. His father's name was Auver, and, in addition to his work on the farm, he was known far and wide for the good shuttles he made. He had made himself a name as a hatmaker, and was clever with his hands. At the age of four, little Sondre lost his mother, and he and his younger brother Eivind – who later became one of Morgedal's best ski makers – grew up in their grandfather's house. The only schooling he had was a few weeks of ambulatory school in the winter, but Sondre learnt to both read and write.

«Around him there was a world full of mountains, steep hills, difficult terrain, precipices, wood for tools, weaver's shuttles, poverty, a strange and difficult ABC, and an inordinate amount of useless reading. But outside, the hills called, and he had to answer. There he inscribed his first turns in the snow and learnt the syntax of skiing . . .» (Loupedalen)

It goes without saying that Sondre had to work hard from an early age to earn his living. In the summer there was haymaking on the steep slopes and hard work in the woods as well as the herds to be looked after. He was small for his age, and thin, but under his clothes his body was muscular, lithe and supple. When there was rivalry in physical prowess Sondre was always one of the contestants, and once he lifted a heavy log chair with one finger. But even though he never gave in he was sometimes beaten by a better man. Once he played finger-tug so hard that his little finger cracked. «Sondre had a bent finger after that day,» remarked Loupedalen laconically.

Aslak Bergland, clergyman and poet, was probably the one who best depicted Sondre's daredevil skiing. He wrote a whole collection of poems, which he called «Garland of Leaves», and many of the poems describe the skiing activities of Morgedal, with Sondre as the central figure. Like this poem about Sondre's wild run down from Kvævenuten:

Behold him on the highest peak,
Adjusting skis and bindings.
With cap in hand he stands erect,
Then plunges boldly down.

You saw him race from steep to steep
With snowdust in his wake,
Now in the air, now on the ground,
Headlong down the hill.

He leapt aloft from off the roof
And floated o'er the barn.
Far down the hill he landed then,
And stopped at Bjaaland's farm.

It was his first great skiing feat,
The run he made that day.
And later there were none who dared
To follow in his tracks.

In the years that followed, the number of daring exploits on skis increased steadily. He travelled round the rural communities making shuttles, and everywhere he went he skied in a way that people had never seen the likes of. Nobody imitated him later on either, for that matter. He also travelled over to Setesdalen and impressed people there with his superb skiing. Even so, his most daring feat was in Morgedal. The Kastedal bluff is not far from Highway E 76 when you drive out of Morgedal on the way west. One winter evening Sondre and his friend Talleiv Kastedalen were on their way home from felling timber, and they stopped at the edge of the steep slopes down Kastedalen, with the lake far below them in the bottom of the valley. Loupedalen has described it like this:

«Shall we ski down here?» said Sondre.

«If you dare to go first, then I'll follow you,» answered Talleiv. Sondre pushed his axe down inside his jacket collar, adjusted his ski bindings, and looked down the hill to ascertain the best course to take.

«Mind you don't cut yourself,» said Talleiv.

«Mind you don't shoot yourself,» replied Sondre – for Talleiv was carrying his gun – and started off down the hill.

On the right
One of the most popular half-documentary films shown on Norwegian televison, was the film about Sondre Norheim. In this film only people from Morgedal took part, and the film showed that the skiers from Morgedal still excelled in both daring and technique. This popular film has been reshown several times since it was produced by Johan Vestly in 1970. The picture to the right was taken by Vestly during the filming in Morgedal.

The large picture at the very front and back of the book are also taken in conjunction with this film.

THE MOUNTAIN SETTLEMENTS OF TELEMARK

«Skiing - the pole-less downhill run, at a speed that makes the earth fade away and the skier take to the air like a bird – and the sudden, steep turns – this inimitable art has been given to us from the mountain settlements of Telemark.»
(Preface in «FORENINGEN TIL SKI-IDRETTENS FREMME 1883–1933»)

When they got down to the houses in Kastedalen, Talleiv fell, but Sondre kept on down the steepest part of all, below the houses and out onto the frozen lake, Moskei. When his skis were hardly moving any longer, he leapt into the air with a great cry.»

Plunging down from steep to steep,
Taking gullies in their stride.
Like a cloud of misty spray,
Snow thrown up behind their skis.
When they got below the houses,
Came the place where Talleiv fell.
Sondre raced on, down and down.
Choosing out his course with care.

Tallev, daring, climbs back up,
Even higher than before.
– Just this slope fills one with awe –
Followed Sondre all the way,
Tracks that others dared not follow,
Sondre puts them all to shame.
N'er again will daring skiers
Conquer Kastedal's steep slopes.

This was how Aslak Bergland described the wild dash down Kastedalen, Sondre's most daring exploit, and one that he never surpassed.

In 1854 Sondre married Rannei Ånundsdotter. They were the same age, 29 years old, and together they were to struggle to build a home and feed a growing family. Responsibility and a sense of duty were not Sondre's strongest personality traits. He only half-finished a lot of work, and both the inhabitants of the community and other people were of the opinion that he was a fool who thought of nothing but skiiing and fun for the kids. The following story illustrates this very well. The poor-law authorities gave him a barrel of seed potatoes, which he planted. Later Sondre admitted that he had dug them up one by one and eaten them for dinner. «When he ran out of wood, he carved chips off the barn wall – that wall must have been replaced a good many times,» said an old Morgedal man. (Loupedalen) Sondre lived in different places, but eventually got hold of the little tenant farm that he called Norheim. Even though it was a good place, with fertile soil, they were just as poor as ever. Rannei was clever with her needle, and she helped out as best she could. But in his craze for skiing, Sondre squandered everything. There must have been many difficult times for the six children – though the whole of the skiing world ought to be pleased about it.

If we think of the billions that have rolled in to the skiing industry as a result of Sondre Norheim's experiments and «nonsense,» we do not need much hindsight to wish that this family had enjoyed a little more prosperity in their lifetime.

But as a skier, Sondre was a better father than most. The children of Morgedal swarmed round him, and he taught them and guided their steps. When he retired from competitive skiing, those who succeeded him at the top of the results lists had one and all had Sondre as both example and teacher.

Interest in skiing in Morgedal from the 1860's on was enormous. Many kept on skiing on the hills even at an advanced age, and «Old Boys» competitions are still being arranged.

Sondre was a legend in his lifetime, with his heyday in the 1960's. But it was not until 1868 that he took part in a competition in the capital, Christiania. Before that the «Skiing Competition at Ofte» was held in Høydalsmo in 1865 or '66. This was the first competition with prizes that we know of, and it was only for local people. Sondre Norheim had been asked to take part just the same, for his dynamic skiing would make it a really splendid event. He won – as everyone had expected – and the first prize was a big grandfather clock. The race had been organized by the doctor in Lårdal, Andreas Bakke, and after the prize distribution he sent the hat round for an extra prize for the competitor who could give the public the most spectacular performance on skis.

THE FOUNDATIONS FOR SKIING ARE LAID

«In these years the first skiers from Telemark came in for the races in Kristiania. Their skiing was like a revelation and showed the way for the whole country. Riding the poles disappeared, the Telemark ski came into use as well as real harnesses, and the sport of skiing was founded.»
(K. Vilh. Amundsen: Skiløpning Kristiania 1924)

Loupedalen tells the story in this way:

'They had cleared a way through the bushes up to the top of a little mountain, Ofte Mountain, which lay above the ski slope.

«How do you feel about it now, Sondre,» he was asked.

«I'm not afraid,» he answered.

«Do you dare to go from the top?»

«You'll see me up there like an eagle,» was the answer.

Others had tried the slope before, and had nasty falls. And the holes they had made in the snow made it particularly difficult to ski there.

The people at the bottom of the hill saw Sondre first when he was actually taking off – it was as though he came from nowhere. Birch and other trees seemed to whistle past him until he got onto the track below, twisting and turning on his skis, supple as ever. He looked dry and skinny with his trousers flapping around him. The snow hissed under his skis on the hard, bumpy hill until he got onto the ordinary track and jumped a long way on that jump, too. He had hardly landed under the jump before he turned sharply in the middle of the slope.'

It goes without saying that Sondre won the extra prize.

Sondre did not become a national figure until he was more than 42 years old, after the competition at Iversløkken in Christiania in 1868. When we remember that Sondre scarcely had enough money for food, and was «as poor as a church mouse» (Loupedalen), the trip to Christiania is a good example of how skiing took priority over everything else. His trip to the capital was paid for. The course went first to Seljord, then up Grunningsdalen and down to Sauland. From Heddal it went over Meheia to Sandsvær and then it was straight to Drammen and Christiania. His knapsack was packed with food prepared by Rannei. He had two friends with him, Olav Ånundsen Drangstveit and Olav Torjusson. They were also to do well in the competition.

It was a competition that was a combination of jumping, cross-country, and what the people of Morgedal called «slalom». Times were recorded for all the competitors, but there were also a number of places round the course where style was judged – and not only jumping style (see page 5). There were more than fifty competitors, from North Østerdalen to Tele-

Upper right
The first ski competition we know about in Kristiania, was arranged at «Eugenie's Foundation's Hill» or Iversløkken by Gamle Aker Church in 1866. Two years later, Sondre Norheim made his breakthrough here. From Iversløkken the competition was moved to Husebybakken and later to Ullbakken. After that began the well-known Holmenkollen competitions.

Lower right
These skiers from Hallingdal had in common with the skiers from Telemark a long way to go to attend the competitions in the capital city. They skied 150 to 250 km each way.

Iversløkken
Sundhell85

15
1
3
2
8
5
10

THE TELEMARK SKI IS PERFECT

«The Telemark ski has been adopted, its lines have been determined, and it has attained a perfection which will hardly be subject to greater changes in the future. The harnesses, one may assume, seem to be on the right track, and footwear and equipment have kept pace with the development in skiing.»
(Fritz Huitfeldt: Skiløbning i text og billeder 1908)

mark, but it was the skiers from Trysil and Morgedal in particular who dominated the competition. The day after, there was a report in the newspaper «Aftenbladet». Most people seemed to have noticed the winner:

«It was the winner of the 1st. prize who excelled over all the other competitors. He has such a remarkable style of skiing that one would think he had been born to it, and that it was his natural way of moving around. With the ski pole like a walking stick in one hand, and his cap in the other, he started off down the hill at top speed – then suddenly he jumped, so that his skis did not touch the ground for 2 or 3 ski lengths. When he landed after such a jump there was not a trace of unsteadiness or lack of balance. Only when one has seen Sondre Ouversen Norheim and recalls that the man is now 43 years old, can one begin to imagine what such a first-class skier would be able to accomplish in his prime.»

The other two from Morgedal also did well in the competition. Here is the results list, which shows that the winners came from all over the country:

1st. prize, worth 10 spd.[1]:
Sondre Ouversen Norheim, Kviteseid.
2nd. prize, worth 8 spd.:
Elling Bakken, Soknedalen.
3rd. prize, worth 6 ½ spd.:
Halvor Halvorsen Skjærberget, Trysil.
4th. prize, worth 5 spd.:
Kadet Jacobsen, Christiania.
5th. prize, worth 4 spd.:
Hans Andreassen, Nordre Land.
6th. prize, worth 3 ½ spd.:
Ole Torjussen Bygland, Kviteseid.

This skiing competition was an enormous breakthrough for Sondre and his style of skiing. There he demonstrated the Telemark turn for the first time, and the parallel turn that was later to become the basic turn in modern alpine skiing and was – surprisingly – given the name Christiania turn in 1901 (see page 12). He showed skiing enthusiasts and competitors his new skis and bindings, the first ones with a heel strap. Three or four competitions later, everybody had this equipment. He showed everyone that he only used one short pole, not the long, thick sticks that many people struggled with, and that were more suited to supporting a hay-drying rack than anything else. It was not just his brilliant idea of waisting his skis that people noticed; they were also much shorter than other skis, only 2.40 metres, whereas others had skis up to 3 metres long. With his short skis he also showed them the «herringbone» technique for going up a hill.

A month later that same winter, on March 8, there was a big competition in Kviteseid. In the subsequent report in the Christiania newspapers, this Haugeli race was held up as an example of the sort of mad skiing that could easily kill you. It had been very mild early in the day, and the snow conditions were not suitable until

[1] spd. = spesi-dollar, a silver coin worth about 8 crowns.

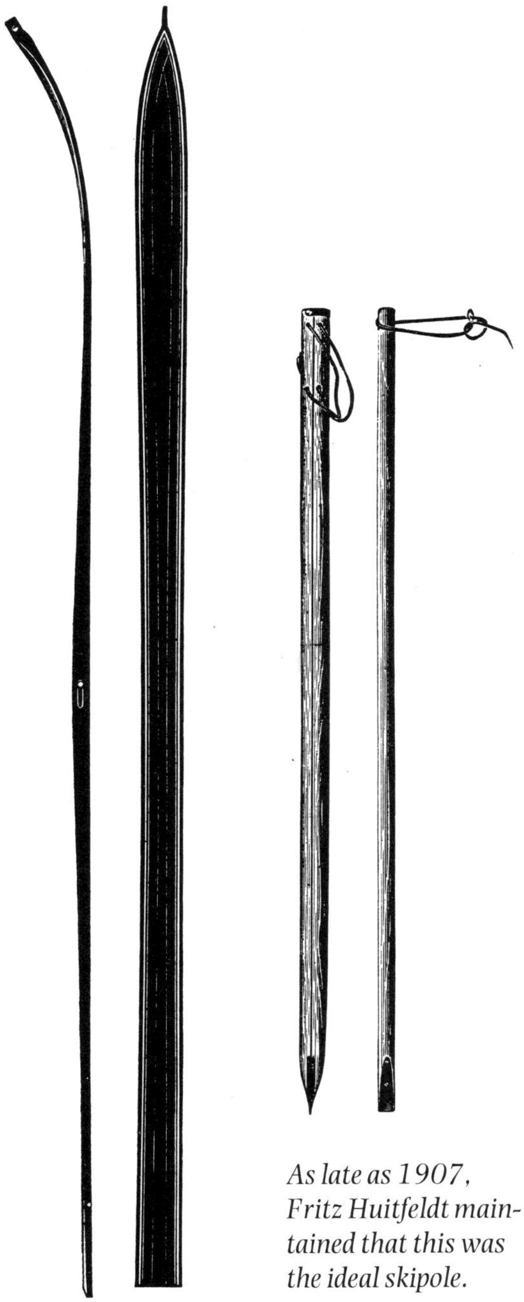

As late as 1907, Fritz Huitfeldt maintained that this was the ideal skipole.

The leading ski manufacturers in Telemark before 1900 were Svein Juve from Seljord, Knut Olavsen Haugen and Åsmund Brekke in Kviteseid. Fritz Huitfeldt combined the best qualities of Sondre Norheim's, Eivind Mostaul's and these ski manufacturers' skis, and made his own model which came to be sold all over the world.

late in the afternoon. This meant that the race had to be finished as fast as possible, and the competitors were allowed to choose the slope they thought would suit them best. The race was held on the steep slopes below Brunkeberg Church, and here there was a steep drop diagonally across part of the course, so that the skiers could choose a big jump or a little jump. From the report in Christiania, we learn that there were seven jumps in the course and three rounds in all. The course consisted of both jumps and downhill stretches. Sondre doubtless tackled more hazardous courses in his time, but he probably never jumped further than here in Haugli. They measured the longest jump as 50 alen - an alen was 0.677 metres. The newspapers, on the other hand, wrote only 30 alen, and even that with some reservations: «The account suffers from a considerable amount of exaggeration.» The newspapers reported for the first time that Sondre skied with his skis strapped to his feet. In the first round he had chosen a difficult slope, which others had also had a go at:

«Many tried after him, but were not so successful. They fell head over heels, so that one would have thought they had broken both arms and legs, but they all came out of it unhurt. One would have thought that Sondre, who is supposed to be the best skier in Telemark, would be satisfied with such a run. But no, in the second round he went to a higher starting-point than had been agreed on, whereby the course became even more difficult, and started off in such a way that even his friends the farmers thought it would be impossible for him to manage such a course.»

But Sondre did manage it, and he now ruled supreme in the world of skiing. In 1870 he went to Christiania with a couple

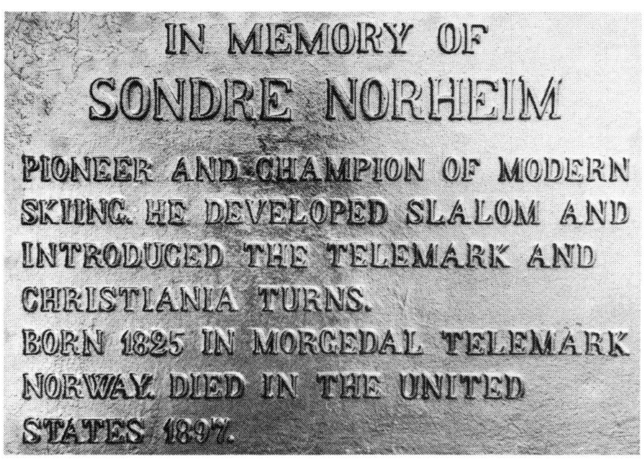

Pam Norheim was on the American National Team in biathlon at the World Championships in Holmenkollen in 1986. At the Ski Museum in Oslo she was told more about what great-grandfather Sondre had done for skiing before he emigrated to the USA in 1884.

Left
Memorial plaque to Sondre Norheim in the USA, with the same text as on the memorial stone in Morgedal.

of men from Seljord and demonstrated his style of skiing. They were given free board and lodging, and persuaded the skiing enthusiasts of the city to organize competitions in the capital. Gradually these skiers learnt a lot from what they saw the Telemark men doing. In one of the reports it said: «At Landingen both of the 'Telemarkinger' won the speed skiing mainly because of their short skis, which allowed them to ski uphill in a way that resembles skating.» It might not have been the skating technique as we know it today, but it was the first description of «herringboning» uphill.

46-year-old Sondre realised that he was

getting older, and the writing on the wall appeared in 1871 at the national competition in Christiania. On the sharp, icy surface it was a spry young man from Seljord, Aslak Smedal, who was all of three minutes faster than Sondre downhill, although they were equally good in the jumping. If we go forward to 1875, Sondre is still competing, at the age of 50. The report says:

«. . . his legs must have become somewhat stiffer than they were before, because despite the fact that he jumped very well, he spent so long on the downhill course that he did not qualify for a prize. However, they decided to give him a 16th. prize of a little object made of silver, together with a 10-crown gold coin.»

Eventually, Sondre had to give up competitive skiing, but he helped the children of Morgedal for many years. He did not run an organized ski school, but he was always willing to give good advice. Olav Bergland told Torjus Loupedalen about this, in connection with a competition on the Møybring slope at Groven. It was a race for adults, but the young boys stood there, itching to take part.

'Sondre caught sight of them and found a 2-crown coin in his purse.

«The kids must have some fun, too,» he said. «This is to be the prize for a race for them.»

And that was what happened. The 2 crowns cost Sondre a lot; he had to go without his favourite drink, coffee, for at least a fortnight.'

Olav, Sondre's second eldest son, went to America in 1878. The letters he wrote home to Norheim must have spoken highly of the rich country in the west, and 6 years later, at the age of 59, Sondre and Rannei left for America with their children. The flat prairie must have been quite a change for someone who was most at home in the hills, but they settled in Dakota. Sondre died in 1897 and he was buried in the cemetery of Norway Church in Denbigh, North Dakota. At home in Morgedal they held a service of remembrance where Gunnar Mandt, a teacher from Vrådal, made a speech:

«Now that we know that the sport of skiing is 'a joyous sign of the times,' a force that unites all parts of the country, nations, peoples and parties in peaceable competition, we must acknowledge Sondre's unique achievement. The ways of Our Lord are strange. Just when doubt and evil omens were about to wreak havoc with our times, along came a man from Morgedal, poor, in threadbare clothes, and helped to create a new climate of optimism.»

It was the country Sondre emigrated to that, 100 years later, saw the renaissance of his style of skiing – which must give today's skiing community in Norway something to think about. But it would undoubtedly have pleased Sondre himself very much.

During the Biathlon World Championship in Oslo in the winter of 1986, a young girl from the American team wanted to visit the Ski Museum in Oslo. She had heard that they had memorabilia of her great-grandfather there. They certainly did – the girl's surname was Norheim and her great-grandfather was Sondre! It would be difficult to find better proof of the fact that we have come full circle.

SPORT AND POLITICS IN THE HUSEBY RACE 1883

When the «Telemarkinger» went to the capital to demonstrate their skiing proficiency, they skied there and back, about 200 kilometres each way. In 1883 the board of the newly-founded Ski Association had arranged for them to be able to take the train from Kongsberg, at reduced price, provided they notified «The Western Railway's Board of Supervisors as well as the Stationmaster at Kongsberg» in good time. Of the 84 competitors in the Huseby race in 1883 no fewer than twenty were from Telemark. There were large cash prizes, and the winner was to receive the King's Cup. The «Telemarkinger» won the majority of the prize money – 600 out of a total of 823 crowns. The results list showed the best of the competitors from Telemark in the following places:

1. Torjus Hemmestveit, Morgedal
2. Mikkel Hemmestveit, Morgedal
3. Halvor Ådalen, Seljord
4. Kristoffer Dalen, Seljord
5. Torkel Dalen, Seljord
6. Åsmund Svalastog, Kviteseid
7. Såmund Hemmestveit, Morgedal
9. Olav Haugann, Morgedal
10. Ole H. Haugann, Morgedal

The prizes were distributed in the Student Union hall by Prince Oscar. But the men from Telemark were not particularly looking forward to meeting a Swedish prince. 1883 was a dramatic year in Norwegian history along the road towards separation from Sweden in 1905. The issue of separate Norwegian consulates and the conflict over the King's right of veto had alarmed people. In the rural communities in particular, royal power and Stockholm's «remote control» of the country were regarded as unworthy and degrading. In Telemark foreign royal power had the same status as an occupying power would have had, and the skiers took this resentment to Christiania with

Above right
From Iversløkken the competition was moved to Husebybakken in 1879. In 1890 there was so little snow that the competition was held at Ullbakken by Frognerseteren, and in 1892, Holmenkollen was ready and competitions were held there.

Lower right
Our Norwegian royal family have always been a focal point at the jumping hill. Here King Haakon and Queen Maud brave the storm.

4367

THE SOFT SHOE AGE IS ENDED

«Mikkel and Torjus marked the watershed in Norwegian skiing. They stand with one foot in the age of Sondre and the other in more modern times. With the old ski equipment and the old skiing technique stretched to the utmost, Mikkel and Torjus became the first ski instructors. But the willow bands and light, thin pinewood skis without any groove underneath were not suited for high jumps on hard-packed jumping-hills. The combined pleasure and working skis disappeared from the picture.

And thereby the soft-shoe age ended in Norwegian ski sports.»
(Torjus Loupedalen: MORGEDAL, Cradle of Skiing, 1947)

them. When they had finished the race, and were tired, they had a drop of the liquor they had brought with them – which was quite understandable, to celebrate their overwhelming superiority on the slopes. Several of them took an extra mouthful, bearing in mind that they were going to mix with the posh people of the city, and a spot of Dutch courage would not come amiss. However the people of the city did not see things in the same way, for Axel Huitfeldt described it like this in «Idrettsbladet» afterwards:

«After the official toasts, when his Royal Highness had left, everyone was free to speak, and the same thing happened as has happened again and again – some of the «Telemarkinger» drink more than they can hold and start to make speeches. Well, one can put up with nonsense in congenial company, but things developed the way they always had before, what we heard was nonsense and disgruntled remarks and – politics. We fail to understand what reasons the people of Telemark can have for being disgruntled. And if they believe they have reasons for dissatisfaction, why do they not stay away? For if they go on like this much longer, there will soon be no-one who misses them any more.»

It is for posterity to decide who was talking politics and who was not. It is probably correct to say that these altercations at the prize distributions had some political significance in the fight for dissolution of the Union. When Huitfeldt and conservative Christiania newspapers reacted so strongly, it was probably a sign that the people of Telemark could not just be lightly dismissed and forgotten about. As early as 1881 Åsmund Grave from Seljord had made a speech at a prize distribution where he had said what he really meant. With so many influential people present it would have been a shame to let such an opportunity pass. But now, in 1883, there were so many more of them who felt the same way:

«Then Høye Nordgarden from Seljord proposed a toast to sport, and in his address he started with Olav Trygvason and ended up with how totally unacceptable the absolute veto was. There was a tre-

The farms in Morgedal were ideally situated for those who wanted challenges on the ski hills.

The brothers, Torjus and Mikkel Hemmestveit had a great deal of influence on the development of skiing in Norway and the USA after Sondre Norheim's era. In 1881, they ran the first ski school in the world in Kristiania. Many of the great skiers who later became famous, received instructions from the Hemmestveit brothers. These two brothers won nearly all the prizes in the 1880's. Mikkel received the King's Cup in 1886, Torjus in 1883 and 1888. In 1888 he also won the first 50 km race to be arranged, before he emigrated to the USA. Here the two brothers along with other skiers took the lead and won competition after competition in many states. Torjus died in Minnesota in 1930, while Mikkel who had gone back to Telemark many years earlier, died in Morgedal in 1958. Both brothers were awarded the Holmenkollen Medal in 1928.

This was Bloch's drawing of the Huseby competition in 1888. The text under the picture was: 1. Long distance race, 2. Abrupt turn. 3. A somersault, 4. A veteran, 5. The decisive moment.

mendous commotion.

'I was on the point of being thrown out,' said Høye Nordgarden, 'but was allowed to stay in the end. There were 20-25 of us from Telemark at the festivities that evening, so it would have been quite a fight, and that must have scared them a bit.'

'Nansen had a good laugh then,' said Mikkel Hemmestveit, who had been standing beside Nansen when this happened.» There is a certain malicious pleasure in

The Norwegian royal family has become a «skiing royal family» for the whole world. To the left we see King Haakon and to the right King Olav, who was an able ski-jumper himself, giving some skiing tips to their grandchildren. In 1923 he finished 4th in the Norwegian championship on the Songebakken jumping hill near Risør.

the way Loupedalen recounts these events, but for the people of Christiania it showed an unbelievable lack of tact towards the royal family.

It is difficult to say whether it was anger – because the «Telemarkinger» had won so many of the prizes - or whether there were political overtones, but the newspaper «Folkebladet» was furious with them:

«And now a short comment on those of the Telemark farmers who were called up to the King to receive His Majesty's (King Oscar's) compliments. These monkeys certainly are impolite. I suppose it is too much to ask that they bow and scrape with the subservience of a courtier, but one can insist that they take their caps off, when their King speaks to them. I noticed two of them in particular, who made no effort at all to take their caps off when they were in front of the royal stand. Not until the King and the Prince had raised their hats and the Queen had nodded in greeting, did these representatives of 'The People's Sovereignty' graciously condescend to raise their caps a little, nod pleasantly, turn their backs on royalty and amble up the hill. A number of people seem to believe that this form of greeting, or rather non-greeting, is the most suitable one – 'there is something very refreshing, national, popular, about such behaviour' say the Ultra-Norwegians.»

The people from Telemark viewed the proceedings somewhat differently. Torkjel Ofteli from Høydalsmo was one of the spectators at the Huseby race that year, and he described the bustling activity and the large number of spectators:

«The field at the bottom of the hill was full of people and horses, and there were little groups of people on the outcrops round about. One could see that the posh people from Christiania were there; there were fat ladies in silk dresses, and young women in Sunday best, and then the strange coachmen who were dressed like the traditional Yule billy-goats - some people thought they were cabinet ministers.»

THE DEVELOPMENT OF CROSS-COUNTRY SKIS

It was the development of the ski that laid the foundations of skiing as a sport for ordinary people. When Sondre Norheim and others from Morgedal started using waisted skis, this made completely different methods of skiing possible. Waisted skis made turning easier, and this, together with Sondre's new heel bindings, laid the cornerstone of modern skiing. Let us have a look at the development of what we know as the «cross-country ski». By this we mean skis that are intended for varying snow conditions, different types of snow, terrain and skiing styles.

Sondre's cross-country skis were wide, with a good bearing surface in deep powder. They were 1.5 cms narrower in the middle than at the tip. But before he had developed the model that resembles modern slalom skis, a great deal of testing and experimenting took place.

«I wish I could make skis that would get me to the bottom,» he is supposed to have said.

There were several tenant farmers in Morgedal at this time who were skillful ski makers. People said that Eivind Mostaul, Sondre's brother, could make two pairs of skis in an evening, provided he had suitable planks. Eivind was said to be a better skimaker than Sondre, but it was Sondre who thought out the design and construction of the skis. The wood they used was often pine, and the skis did not have a groove underneath. However, as the soft pine skis became worn, natural grooves appeared in the wood. But as people started to jump further and further, the skimakers began to look for other types of wood. Landing on pine skis after a jump of 20–25 metres on the groomed Huseby jump was hard. So they experimented with elm and oak and ash, and Sondre's first triumph on waisted skis was on a pair made of ash. A number of wealthy people down in Kviteseid had become very interested in what these young men from Morgedal were doing. Mathias Rye Florentz and his father, who was the retired local bailiff, had both been bitten by the skiing bug. So in 1870 they asked Sondre to come to their farm, Roeid, and make pairs of skis out of some ash planks they had lying around. Torjus Loupedalen writes about this in his book about Morgedal: «When they had been planed smooth, he rubbed fat into them. Then he scraped soot from the pans and rubbed this in. This

THE DISASTER IN FALUN

«Falun 1974 was the decisive disaster which alienated the skilled craftsman from ski production («ski» means a piece of wood). When the trails became mahine-prepared the snow feeling disappeared as well. The result was a marathon on sleigh runners.»
(Nils Faarlund in «Snø og Ski» No. 1/85)

black colour was exceptionally hard-wearing. Then he made white grooves on the top surface of the skis with a bradawl. Sondre and his brother Eivind (Mostaul) were the first ones to do that in this district, I think. The tips of Sondre's skis were long and resembled a swan's neck, and had notches cut into them both on top and underneath.»

These were skis that other people copied, so that they became known further afield. The carpenter Knut Olavsen Haugen entered a pair of skis he had made for an exhibition in connection with the Huseby race in 1879. The skis, which were based on Sondre's prototype, won first prize and were sold for 20 crowns. The buyer was the lawyer Aksel Huitfeldt, who, incidentally, was well-known as an ardent opponent of women on skis (see page 51). His brother Fritz, whose skis and bindings were later to become internationally famous, went to Telemark at Christmas 1882 to learn more about why the people of Telemark were such superior ski-makers and skiers. Fritz Huitfeldt believed that Knut Olavsen Haugen from Kviteseid was the best skimaker of his time. Haugen's skis served as a model for Huitfeldt's skis, which 14 years later won a gold medal at an exhibition arranged by the Association for the Furtherance of the Sport of Skiing. This model found its way to all four corners of the world, and its trademark, the little «sugarlump» on the tip of the ski, was the symbol of quality Norwegian skis. Thousands of pairs were sold, many of them in the USA. (See page 61.) They were massproduced there for 30–40 years from the turn of the century.

Christian Lund from Nydalen in Oslo started as an apprentice, then in 1910 he established his own business. In 1911 he inserted this advertisement in the Minneapolis Tidende: «Skis made of genuine green ash, Florida magnolia together with toe bindings, the same as Huitfeldt's, with Høier-Ellefsen tightening apparatus, recognized everywhere as the best and most practical skiing equipment in the world. Send for free illustrated catalogue with the lowest prices.»

Up to that time the Telemark ski had outclassed all the other models that had been experimented with. But as early as the 1890's it had become clear that the Telemark cross-country skis were not suitable for all the increased specialisation that was taking place. People were jumping further and further, and demanding hardwood skis that stood up to the landing. The longer cross-country races became, the narrower they made the

Above to the right
One of the well know ski factories was in Gol in Hallingdal. Mekkel Rustberggaard made both cross-country skis and jumping skis, and relics from the ski factory are to bee seen in a little ski museum in Pers Hotel at Gol.

Bottom right
When the Åsnes brothers went back to Straumsnes from Kristiania in 1922, they started to produce skis at home in an old raftered building. Today Åsnes skis are delivered throughout the ski world.

skis. But they kept the proportions that had been Sondre's stroke of genius – widest at the tip, a little narrower at the tail, and narrowest of all in the middle.

In 1904 it was the competitors from Trysil who made a clean sweep of the cross-country prizes at Holmenkollen – and the reason was the skis they used, made by the carpenter Johan Opseth. They were narrower than other skis, and were the first in the world to be made of two different types of wood. Onto the main part of the ski, made of spruce, he had glued a sole made of hard hickory, which gave a good sliding surface, and the spruce made the ski light.

When Roald Amundsen went to the South Pole in 1912 he had hickory skis with him. Olav Bjaaland from Morgedal, who was a national figure because of his skiing achievements, was also a member of the expedition. He was mainly responsible for the skis and sledges, and made sure that the equipment was in top condition all the time. After the expedition Roald Amundsen made the following statement: «We felt a lot of affection for our skis.»

In 1933 Hans Ullevålseter patented the SPLITKEIN method. Laminated skis, consisting of several pieces of wood glued together, did not warp so easily, and if one glued other types of wood under the sole, on the sides, and on the top, one could obtain other advantages.

To the left
The old Telemark skis are still being produced in Morgedal. There is a natural connection between building traditions, applied art and craftsmanship and the design of skis.

To the right
The Åsnes factory utilizes both old tradition and new technology to keep up with the hard competition.

This patent also helped to establish the American ski industry. Peter Østby took over the patent rights of the SPLITKEIN method, and sold licences to two other Norwegians in the USA, Thor Groswold in Denver and Christian Lund of the Northland factory in St. Paul, Minnesota. When the Germans occupied Norway in 1940, the export of skis from the country stopped. But in the USA the military needed everything that Groswold, Northland and Splitkein could produce, and after the war more than 20,000 soldiers had been on skis made according to Ullevålseter's patent – yet another Norwegian ski pioneer.

The ski factory that managed on its own

In 1910 the eldest of a family of nine children left Ytre Åsnes at Straumsnes on Dalsfjord. He left for Christiania and quite by chance began to work in a ski factory. Three years later, four of the six Åsnes brothers had begun to work in the factory. Together the brothers gained such insight into the production of skis that they took their expertise home with them in 1922, and started a ski factory in an old raftered building from 1696. Straumsnes had enough snow for skiing about fourteen days of the year, so it was hardly a natural site for ski production. The brothers rowed

«NOT JUST THE BODY, BUT THE SOUL AS WELL»

«Can you imagine anything freer and more exciting than when you, swiftly as a bird, zoom down the wood-clad hillsides while country air and spruce twigs whiz by your cheeks and eyes; brain and muscles are tense, ready to avoid any unknown obstacle which any moment might be thrown in your path? You are one with your skis and nature. This is something that develops not only the body but the soul as well, and it has a deeper meaning for a people than most of us perceive.»
(Fridtjof Nansen 1890

across the fjord and bought ash trees and after some time obtained machines which made the work easier. At the side of the yard a stream went through the mill-house, and they constructed a belt transmission from the waterwheel across the yard to the ski factory!

Sixty years later, Åsnes Ski Factory was the only Norwegian factory which took the Telemark renaissance in the USA seriously. This was at the end of the 1970's, and they started production of the model MT-54 in the early eighties. By this time the factory had made its mark as the producer of many good mountain and touring ski types, and felt that they were highly competent in the field of cross-country skis. In 1977 the factory sold 136,500 pairs of skis and reached its peak before the declining market caught up with them as it had done with Landsem, Madshus and all the other factories. In 1975 there were 13 ski factories in Norway, today there are 3 left. Åsnes hit the bottom in 1982 with only 34,000 pairs of skis sold. Then the Telemark style came back and created new optimism, with more than a doubling of production during the next three years. It is quite indicative of the difficulties in ski production that Åsnes Ski Factory is the only factory which has not gone through bankruptcy, legal settlements or been held alive by some bigger company. However, the conflict between old ski traditions and modern technology has created tough competition conditions the last twenty years. Particularly after central European and American ski giants threw themselves into the production of touring and cross-country skis.

The fact that the Åsnes factory is especially mentioned here is also to show that a purely family concern can attain international recognition. Everyone working in the factory is either from the Åsnes family or from the neighboring farms. Together they have built up a highly technical ski industry which makes skis for the whole world, and if they had not received the new thrust forward with the Telemark renaissance, it might have led to the depopulation of Straumsnes.

Many of the ski craftsmen at factories like Landsem, Madshus and Åsnes went against their will into the new technology with materials like acryl, aluminium, polyethylene and fiberglass after 1974. As one of them said: «When the building industry goes away from steel constructions in large buildings and over to laminated roof beams of glued wood, we go in the opposite direction, away from Splitkein skis of wood and over to runners made by American astronauts.»

To the right
Mountain skiing makes strict demands on equipment, and robust cross-country skis are the only ones which hold in weather and terrain like this.

26

FISCHER
ATOMIC
ARC
TELEMARK
MADSHUS
TE 35
KÄSTLE
ELAN
EXPEDITION
BLIZZARD
DYNASTAR
LANDSEM
DURET
KARHU
SKILOM
Touring 135
åsnes
ROSSIGNOL

Skis for cross-country skiing

There can be many reasons for the new upsurge of interest in Telemark skiing, which took place in the USA first in the 1970's. The main positive side of this is the increased interest in cross-country skis; skis which are steady and good when we go through the mountains with knapsacks on our backs, skis which turn well, which have steel edges that ensure a firm grip on icy hills and which have the right balance between tension and curvature. Unless the ski trails are as narrow as streetcar tracks, these cross-country skis can also be used in prepared trails. And last but not least it is tempting to use them for skiing among trees and bushes, in the woods and hills and in open country. But with cold, loose snow conditions, the new Telemark skis are rather too narrow. Then broad, inward curving, mountain skis constructed according to the Norheim/ Huitfeldt model are better as they run on top of the soft snow. However, the difference in weight causes most people to refrain from using these heavier skis.

After the new interest in the Telemark turn in the USA the Telemark skis have become the new cross-country skis for varied use. They are narrower than the old ones, but perform very well both in loose snow and on prepared hills. The Norwegian Åsnes skis, MT-54 TELEMARK can serve as an example, as they are the ones most used in this country. These are laminated fiberglass skis, but have a nucleus of genuine Norwegian spruce. Thus there is Norwegian natural material in the ski itself and American «chemistry» on the outside – in the coating and steel edges. The sides are of polyurethane and the bottom of polyethylene. They are not as good in loose snow as the Sondre skis, but nevertheless they are in accordance with the ski cultural roots from Telemark. In addition they are stable under icy conditions and on hard prepared hills.

To the left
This collection of Telemark skis were presented in Ski Star *the winter of 1986. Some are intended for competitions, others for cross-country skiing, so it is best to seek advice concerning which model to choose. There are also American, Japanese and other European Telemark models.*

All over the ski world the production of Telemark skis is «big business» and a pop-trend with many facets. Already in 1981, Steve Barnett wrote in the magazine «CROSS-COUNTRY»: «The Telemark revolution has gone too far.» The equipment has become too similar to alpine equipment, with high boots of the Alpine type and with big Telemark competitions which have become more and more like slalom competitions with parallel turns. (See page 78.)

However it is the positive «anti-movement» in the USA which should make us rejoice. The «Back-Country» style or the «Cross-Country» style as it could be called, has drawn the ski industry after it. In 10–15 years the production of so-called «all-round» skis had multiplied. With these skis many of the ski enthusiasts have moved away from the well-prepared slope to the back of the hill where the snow is not packed down and where there are no trails like streetcar tracks in the snow. Competition skiers have their own models and «cross-country» people theirs. But all are in accordance with the Telemark idea.
At this point it may be appropriate to discuss what we should look for when we are buying skis of the Telemark type. (The following information is based on conversations with skiers, people who sell skiing

THE ESSENCE OF SKIING

«The ski specialist, whether it be in jumping or in cross-country races, knows only a part of skiing. Life on skitrips, the experience of living with nature, fast and daring skiing in difficult and varied terrain – this is the essence of skiing and its freshest source.»
(Amundsen)

equipment, and also from the catalogue of Scandinavian Mountain Skiing Equipment in Hemsedal.)

1. The length of the skis should be about 25 cm bigger than your own height.
2. The tension should be such that the skis perform well in loose snow, but at the same time retain their wax on hard surface snow. The measuring stick for this is that without any excessive effort you should be able to bend the ski with one hand.
3. The curvature on the sides should be altogether at least 10 mm. (The difference in width at the curve and in the middle of the ski.)
4. The metal used on the edges should be of steel.
5. The skis must be stiff when you try to twist them.
6, The ratio between the tension and the curvature is important. Put the bottom end of the ski on the floor, take hold of the tip and squeeze the ski in the middle. If the «reversed» bow is even, you have a good Telemark ski . . . assuming that the other requirements are fulfilled.

It is quite gratifying, therefore, that the Åsnes Ski Factory with its rich traditions has made a model which skiers consider fulfills all these requirements.

Curvature and width of cross-country skis from 1850 to today

King Haakon's touring skis	8.8	7.6	8.2
Stein Eriksen's Olympic skis	8.6	7.2	7.7
Hemmestveit ski	8.5	7.1	7.6
Huitfeldt's model	8.5	7.2	7.6
Sondre-Norheim-ski	8.4	6.9	7.6
Skis for climbing	8.2	7.0	7.5
Mountain skis	7.2	6.1	6.8
Light cross-country/ mountain skis	6.5	5.5	6.0
Åsnes MT-54 Telemark	6.3	5.4	5.9

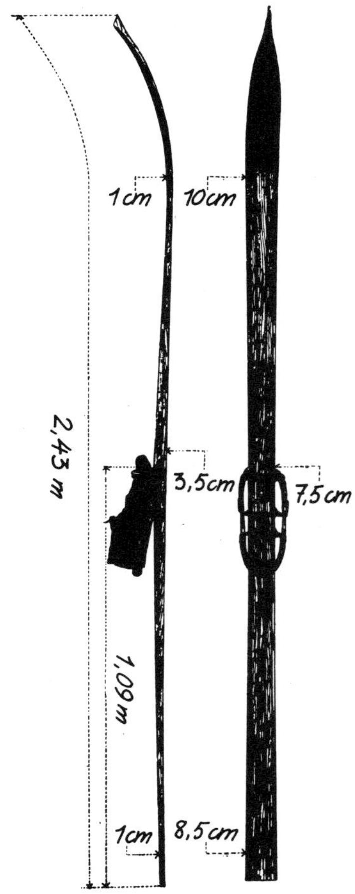

There are still those who maintain that the Telemark skis are the ideal skis in loose snow across open country.

Boots for cross-country skiing

The turning technique for Telemark skiers differs from the slalom technique in that you ski with the heel free. Whether one uses wire-bindings of the Kandahar type or toe-harnesses such as Rottefella, the boots are subjected to extreme stress when skiing downhill.

From the turn of the century and up to the 1960's it was customary to use sturdy ski-boots in wire harnesses for mountain and cross-country skiing. Around 1970 there was a demand for skis and boots to be both thin and light, and thereby competition equipment for special long distance competitions came into a field they should never have entered. Both skis and boots were specially made for pre-prepared trails, and they were dangerous for varied ski conditions in the mountains.

People have gradually become aware of this, and now ski enthusiasts are more adept in choosing safe and correct mountain equipment.

With the Telemark skiing from the USA came the producers, with varied types of «Telemark-Boots», a warm, sturdy and stable ski boot. Now the material was also so light that the transition from thin cross-country boots wasn't nearly as dramatic.

The new boots are to be had in various models. Both in height, quality, weight and stiffness there are many models to choose between. If one is doing competition Telemark skiing, higher special boots are required. For mountain use stricter demands for heat insulation are necessary and it is important that they are watertight.

The sole on the Telemark boots is stiff on the sides, so that it doesn't twist in the Rottefella harnesses as the long-distance boots do. At the same time it is soft enough lengthwise that it bends easily in the toe-harness. The sole should be at least 15 mm thick, so that it insulates well. The best to be had are welted leather soles with glued in Vibram rubber soles. In order to insert this boot into the toe harness, it is necessary to have a special Telemark harness of the Rottefella type. These harnesses can take soles which are between 12 and 20 mm thick. The toe shackle on these harnesses is of flat spring steel and therefore spares the sole edges of the boots.

The boots should be high enough to give good ankle support. This is not only important for making turns and skiing easier. It also helps to prevent the ankle being damaged by skiing in loose snow.

The new sturdy ski boots are to be had in many types. The Norwegian Alfa factory has made a model which many Telemark skiers use, and the Italian Asolo factory makes a number of different models with Telemark as a trademark. Had Sondre and other skiers from Morgedal been told that their skiing would be keeping Italian shoe production going a hundred years later, they would have just laughed. The sturdy boots are extremely light and give good supprt for skiing in all kinds of terrain.

Toe-straps of willow or of leather date back to pre-historic time. They were used with toe-socks of leather which were bent into a corner at the toe.

It was therefore easy to kick off the skis when hunting, herding reindeer or working in the woods.

The toe-strap binding date back to the 18th century. Willow-straps went over the toe-cap and a little loop went under the foot-sole. The bindings could also be made of thick rope or a small block of wood fastened onto the skis right behind the toe-strap.

The willow toe-strap and heel-binding were known from around 1850. The foot was fastened firmly to the ski, and thereby it was easier to steer the skis. It was this binding and the skis with the curved in sides which formed the basis for the development of modern skiing, and both were developed in the skiing milieu around Sondre Norheim.

The cane-bindings came in the 1880's. Gunnerius Schou took out a patent on them, and it is the first patent to be taken on ski equipment altogether. Canes with leather bound around them were screwed firmly to the skis.

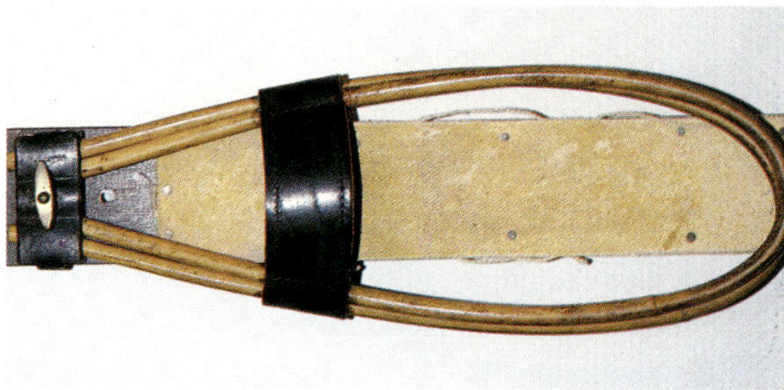

The cane-binding appeared around 1890 from L. H. Hagen's factory in Kristiania. This binding was an important step toward a binding which fitted different feet and boots.

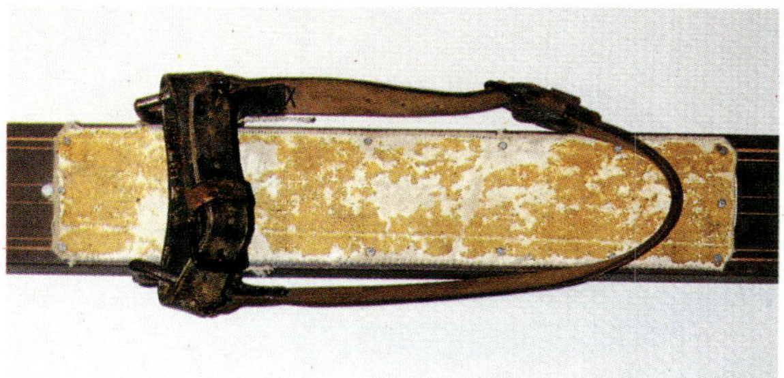

In 1894, Fritz Huitfeldt took out a patent on the first binding with an iron lug on each side of the ski. A strap was fastened to this lug to tie around the heel.

In 1897, Huitfeldt made an alteration by having a piece of iron punched through the hole in the strap and bent up on both sides.

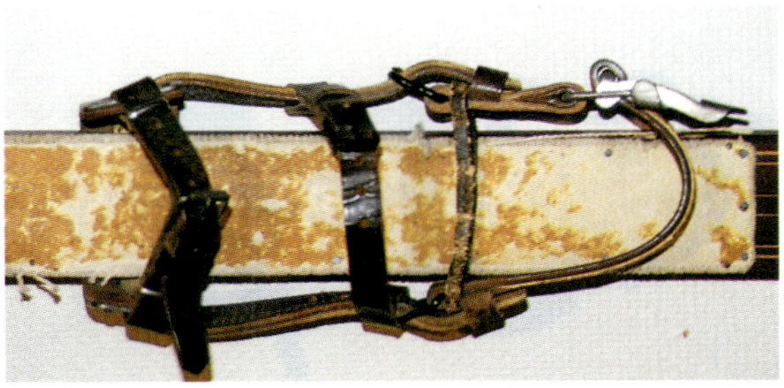

The next Huitfeldt binding included a Høyer Ellefsen tightener which was modelled on the bottle corks of that time! This combination became one of the most important bindings in the world up till about 1930.

In 1920 Marius Eriksen, Stein Eriksen's father, took out a patent on a toe-harness fastened onto the ski, such as we have on the Kandahar harnesses today.

The cross-country bindings developed in their own direction from around 1890. This was one of the first on the way toward specialization.

This binding from around 1900 has a toe-harness which can be regulated. Otherwise it has iron over to the toe-strap and a heel-binding of leather.

This is the Bergendahl binding. In 1913, Olaf Selmer patented the first cross-country binding.

Fritz Huitfeldt also made his own binding with toe fastener. This is from 1920.

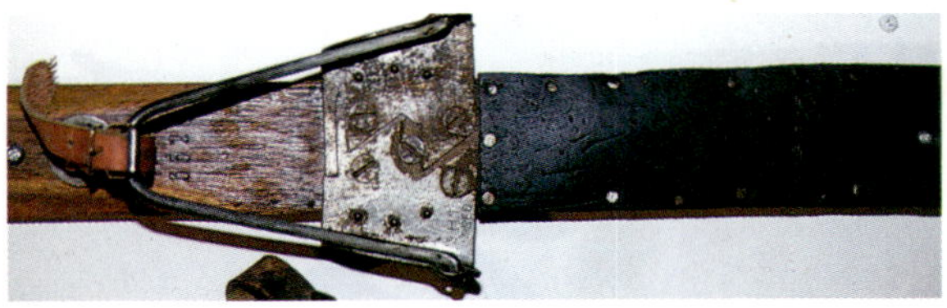

In 1927, Bror With invented an exceptional binding which gradually spread all over the skiing world. The patent he took out then was called the Rottefella (Rat-trap), and here is the first model.

The Rottefella model was further developed by With, and this is the model from 1932. This binding was so brilliant, that even today it is the dominating toe-harness for the whole world. The model Super Telemark came in 1984, and it is the one most used for terrain and Telemark skiing.

TELEMARK-COMBINATION

Jumping – Slalom – Cross-Country Races

Many of the ski competitions in Telemark in the 1860's were a combination of all three disciplines – jumping, slalom and cross-country races. The meet started with the jump and after landing the skier continued from the outrun onto a trail about three km long. Along this trail there were down-hills and these were called slalom.

Torjus Hemmestveit received the King's Cup when he won the first 50 km race ever held in the world.

1888.

Ski-Rend

50 Km.

For at opmuntre Ungdommen til en fornuftig Træning og en rigtigere Forstaaelse af Skiløbningens Nytte har en Privatmand opstillet en Præmie til en Værdi af 400 Kr. for **et Længdeløb paa omtr. 50 Km.**, udført i Aaret 1888 efter Regler og Bestemmelser, der senere vil blive bekjendtgjort.

Rendet vil blive afholdt under Ledelse af

Foreningen til Ski-Idrættens Fremme.

Christiania, Decbr. 1886 (323)

For the first Huseby competition in 1869 the rules clearly stated that the three disciplines would be judged equally. The highest score combined was 3.0. The best time, the best jump and landing, one point, and the same was given for the best style in turns and on the trail.

In Seljord in Telemark combined competitions in jumping and slalom were arranged during the winter of 1886. Mikkel Hemmestveit took part, but didn't get a prize because he had a fall in the slalom. Fifty years later he was interviewed by a Skien newspaper and related: «When I was a boy, jumping was combined with slalom. This was actually long before we started cross-country skiing and combined it with jumping. I remember very well the first time I was in a competition with prizes on the well-known Donstad hill in Morgedal when I was 8 or 9 years old. That was in 1871 or 1872. First they jumped three times, and then there was slalom. The slalom course was at the edge of the hill out over some high cliffs and down over some steep humps. There weren't any stakes or markers to show you where to go. You just had to set out from the top of the hill.

In the same year, in 1886, there came a

proposal to the Ski Association that the skiers should be required to use the same pair of skis for jumping and for cross-country. The committee did not agree to this, but in 1899 the proposal was put forward again, this time from Bærum Ski Club. But again the committee did not agree, for already then skis began to be specialized. At the annual general meeting of the Ski Association in 1900, there was considerable discussion and many claimed that it was high time to get rid of these detrimental specialization tendencies in ski sport before it was too late. But here again the proposal of one pair of skis for both jumping and cross-country was rejected.

Mikkel Hemmestveit was two years younger than Torjus. He came back from Amerika and lived in Morgedal until he died at 95 years of age.

At the Holmenkollen meet in 1895, combined cross-country and jumping had gained the upper hand as a skiing combination, but nevertheless slalom was made part of the cross-country course:

«The course did not follow Gamleveien down to Tryvandene, but down the slope southward over some steep hills where the slalom was located and judges posted. The trail led straight across Skaadalen up on to the bogs toward Skjennungen, where the unfortunate skiers were forced up to the top so that they could be criticized when they came down on the other side by way of another slalom. It looked as if the trail should go by way of Slagteren, but it didn't do that. It went off to the south east and presented another parallel, a side line of the Frøensvoldskleiva, where a new slalom went in twists and turns and caused difficulties for many of the skiers.

Six years later, in 1901, rules came into force which made the combined competition into the pattern we have today. The new rules brought about comformity between the points for the jumping competition and the cross-country times. If a skier jumped poorly, he could reckon out how many seconds or minutes he had to make up in the cross-country competiton. In the jumping event, the correct Telemark style was still important, both in the start, the jump, the landing and the final finishing swerve on the outrun. The landing had to be the well-known Telemark landing, but on the outrun either the Christiania turn with parallel skis could be used, or the Telemark turn with one leading ski in front of the other. This was what was left of the Telemark combination from the 1860's, or the classic SKIATHLOM if we prefer that therm.

GIRL SKIERS

Girls have been skiing as long as the boys, but the sex role patterns in the middle of the nineteenth century were no better than today. So while Sondre Norheim and others could fool around on the ski hills, the women had to look after the homes or simply the Sunday dinner. Far back in the years 1518–19 Bishop Olaus Magnus drew a map with a picture of a woman on skis. The map came out in 1539.

The clergyman Hans Jacob Wille has described women in Seljord 200 years ago: «Everywhere there are very few attractive women to be seen, as the majority have big hands and feet and broad hips. The art of pleasing is quite unknown to them, but on the other hand they are all the more resistant to cold, heavy work and strenuous exercise. Quite a few are good at skiing, are extremely strong and can wrestle with men and even beat them.»

If we proceed to P. Chr. Asbjørnsen, he recounts that «At Christmas or on other occasions, when roads are impassable, both women and men go to parties on skis.» Accounts of women on skis are to be found in the works of both Aa. O. Vinje and Jørgen Moe.

Henrik Ibsen from Telemark was not particularly interested in skiing. His only

To the right
The new Telemark skiing is popular with both sexes. Here at Finse in April, 1986 there were more girls than boys at a weekend course for ski enthusiasts who wanted to learn the Telemark technique. If you want to master the technique, attending a ski school is the best way to learn it.

«THEY HAD TO DIG HIM OUT AGAIN»

«Slalom is a concept which is probably known by very few outside of Telemark. It is a downhill race which cannot be arranged on our usual prize competition hills, as they are too short and too uniform. I have only seen such a hill at one single place, and that was at Raukleiv in Seljord in Telemark. One of the local skiers told me that he came off the top «ufs» (cliff) at such a speed that he went right to the bottom in the loose snow, and his comrades literally had to dig him out again.» (Fritz Huitfeldt: Skiløbning i text og billeder 1908)

Girls on the ski-trails in 1906.

skier is a woman, Solveig, who is looking for Peer Gynt in the mountains: «I have been skiing from place to place, I have asked my way; when they tried to find where I was going, I answered: I am on my way home.»

The breakthrough for organized ski sports for women came in Steinkjer. On March 14, 1889, 23 women in the town came together to start a skiing group. A majority vote gave the ski club the name SKADE after the ski goddess in Old Norse mythology. But even though she was the best known ski star in the world of the gods, SKADE lived a very immoral life. This caused one of the women to vote against the name. SKADE, according to mythology, was said to have had a son with Odin, even though she was married to Njård. Hardly any ideal for women a hundred years ago. However the name SKADE was kept.

Opposition from men was massive. Axel Huitfeldt had been chairman of the Ski Association and was the brother of Fritz, whose ski-harness was known all over the world. Axel was a supreme court lawyer and furious at the ski-ladies who filled Frognerseteren after the opening in 1890. Some of the ladies even took a glass of beer to quench their thirst after a two hour trip from the city. Others had the nerve to warm their legs by the fire. Morgenbladet wrote in 1893:

«One lady downs two whole mugs of beer, another stretches her legs into the fire-place to warm them, and even crosses them, and others break the laws of femininity by drinking cognac on the bleachers during the skiing competition.»

But one woman objected strongly. This was Eva Nansen, a well know singer and a good skier. And there is no need to conceal the fact that she was also known by every-

Ski competition for girls in Asker, 1897.

one as Fridtjof Nansen's wife. She wrote among other things:

«It is a crime against the young girls just growing up that their greatest enjoyment, which brings them so much health and vitality should now be degraded. I am sure that if the men who without any consideration have trampled with their wooden shoes upon this enjoyment, knew how much harm they have done, they would have left the whole matter alone. I must admit that I am delighted to meet young girls of our time, when they come skiing along with their rosy, beautiful faces beaming with joy and freshness and health as they come in toward the city after their ski trips. I believe that anyone with any common sense must agree that young girls of our time as a rule have other and more invigorating interests, have other and loftier thoughts than girls 15 years ago. Naturally this is not just because of the skiers, but they, too, and a freer life out in nature, both summer and winter, have undoubtedly contributed considerably to this. However, if this is so, then it really is a shame that attempts are being made to destroy this way of living which should be our strength and glory. Can anyone seriously claim that ladies become more immoral by going skiing, even if they ski with men? Does anyone believe that Kristiania's ballrooms, streets and cafés are in moral respect healthier places for young girls to spend their time in, than the fields and woods around Kristiania?

Altogether it would certainly be worthier of men, and they would be doing themselves and the generations to come, a greater service, if they tried to the best of their ability to support and encourage women's skiing instead of putting obstacles in their way, even if it demanded a slight sacrifice on their part.»

A great contrast is to be observed in Henrik Angell's experience on a ski trip

from Bergen to Kristiania in 1884:

«On the way I only met a group of young girls on their way back from the local minister's. They were all on skis, the one after the other, and all were wearing short black skirts and red stockings. In their red, green or blue mittens they carried their hymn books and catechisms, both wrapped up in a handkerchief, which had obviously not ever been used for anything else.»

In Morgedal there was a skiing competition for girls in 1878. Margit Kvålseth has later recounted that a number of tradesmen, who bought up girls' hair in the various districts, had given a summer scarf with roses on as a prize. Margit was only 8 years old and had to compete in the slalom race, while the older girls were allowed to jump.

Skiing was a real social revolution for city girls. While girls in Morgedal and other places in Telemark played on skis with loose skirts together with the boys on Sundays, it was the struggle against prejudices and corsets which made skiing a more serious matter for the girls in the city.

Top left
Good results in international ski competitions have always led to increased interest in skiing. With Inger Bjørnbakken in Badgastein in 1958, came a new breakthrough for Norwegian alpine sport. She showed like Stein Eriksen, that it was possible to keep up with the alpinists from Central Europe. Before the war Laila Schou Nilsen had won many competitions, but with Bjørnbakken alpine sport was given a new impetus.

Bottom left
A picture of old sex roles? The children are at any rate from Kristiania in 1907.

To the right
At least there is no more of this – special tickets for women!

They had to wear long dresses and corsets. However gradually more sensible skiing styles came to the front. Nevertheless, there was a great outcry when some girls dared to appear in knee-pants after an English model of 1910. That progress came slowly is indicated by the fact that girls for a long time were not allowed to take part in competitions. In cross-country racing it was not before modern times that women were allowed to participate. But nevertheless, Laila Schou Nilsen, Borghild Niskin and Inger Bjørnbakken have written their names in the history of skiing after their contribution on an international level in slalom. After the breakthrough for Norwegian women's cross-country competition in 1966, there has been no stopping them. Today Norwegian women's cross-country competitions are by many considered even more exciting than men's competitions.

NORWEGIAN SKI-TRAILS, THE FIRST IN AMERICA

In 1825, the «Restaurationen» left Stavanger and headed for America. On board were 52 emigrants, poor families filled with hope of a future in the new world. In the next hundred years almost 800,000 Norwegians followed after them. Among them were the most promising of our ski pioneers: Sondre Norheim, Mikkel and Torjus Hemmestveit, Lars and Anders Haugen, and many, many others. The first pioneers left many years previously.

Two young men in Veggli in Numedal put on their skis in the late winter of 1836, and it was not to go hunting in the mountains. They wanted to cross the mountains on skis, in order to get to Stavanger.

Reports and letters from the family in the States told of exceptionally good circumstances for ordinary people. Many young people from small farms which were too small to be divided up, packed their America trunks and set off for the America boat. Ole and Anstein Knudsen Nattestad set out from Numedal April 6, 1936, and travelled first over the mountains to Telemark. They came down to Austbygde in Tinn and spent the night at the Tosteinsen family's home on the small Rui property. There the whole family sat during the evening and listened to the two brothers tell about how great it was in the States. Ten year-old Jon was the one who listened most intently. Little did he know that he would be the great ski pioneer in «the new world» and that his memory is alive today, in the memorial erected to him in 1975. This monument in honour of Snowshoe Thompson is five meters high and stands 2,000 meters above sea-level, between California and Nevada.

It was Anstein Knudsen Nattestad who, when he came back to Norway the year after, lured the Tosteinsen family over to America. While he was in the USA, he and his brother used skis during the winter when they tried to find land for themselves near Beaver Creek, and on Rock Prairie at Beloit near Chicago. After these two, skis

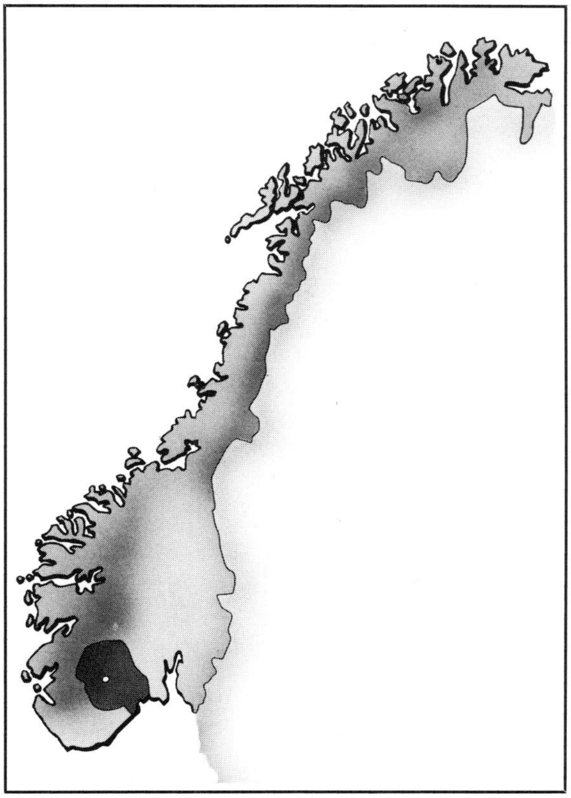

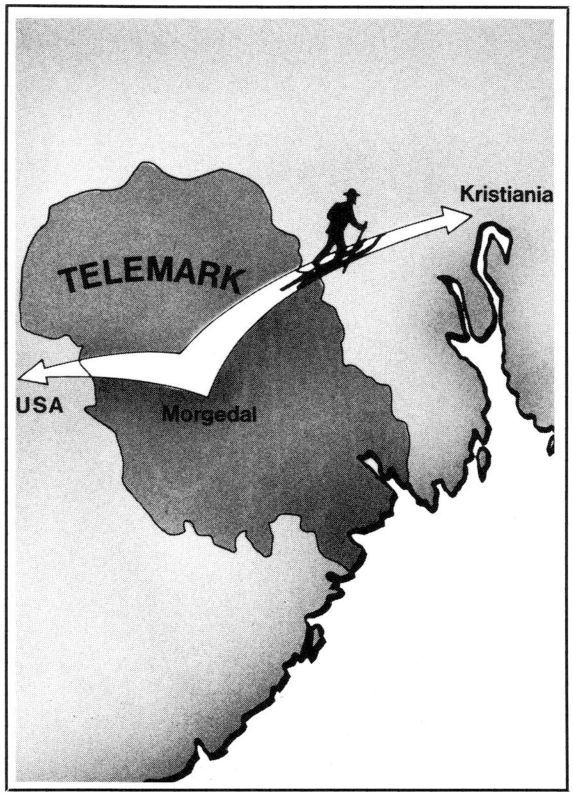

At the Ski Museum in Oslo both the Norwegian public and foreigners are well informed about the saga of skiing. As these two maps show, the first ski trails went from Telemark to Kristiania, and from there over to America with the emigrating skiers.

became more and more used, and in winter were often substituted for snowshoes. Innumerable stories are told of feats accomplished by Norwegians on skis. They started ski competitions as early as 1863, and started with ski waxes long before it was thought of here at home. They often made their own skis themselves and many good ski constructors made their own special models.

Snowshoe Thompson

In connection with Jon Tosteinsen's death in 1876, an American newspaper wrote about him in his obituary: «Snowshoe Thompson was the one who went in front, the mail-coach and freight train and aeroplane came after.» Jon had grown up in Austbygde in Tinn in Telemark, and when he was ten years old, the family emigrated from the tenant farm, Rui, to the country where tenants became landowners themselves. Jon's mother became a widow when he was only three years old, and with 11 brothers and sisters and half brothers and sisters there wasn't a great deal to go around. The family went along with a group of about fifty from Tinn, and they settled at Fox River in Illinois. Later they went along with Cleng Peerson to Missouri and in 1846 we find the Rui brothers among the ones who founded the hardy Blue Mond settlement in Wisconsin.

Jon was an adventurer, so when he got to hear that many people were going to

EXTREMES AND MADNESS

«Often fathers and club leaders want to see their sons and youngsters compete in racing togs and with a starting number on their chests at a very early age. This can lead to un-sporty behaviour and poor losers.

On the other hand, it is not wrong to arrange a meet now and then, to stimulate them. But let these competitions be a really special event.»
(Einar Bergsland: Norsk Skiløpning idag 1940)

California to get rich quickly as gold-diggers, he tagged along. He now called himself John Albert Thompson. This was around 1850. However, the whole picture had changed. California was flooded with people who wanted to search for gold, at times there were almost 100,000 of them. Jon didn't find the gold he had expected, for one day when he saw a poster announcing that the authorities were looking for a strong and vigorous individual to take on a new postal route right across Sierra Nevada, he signed on straight away. In the summer the mail went by mail-coach and used no more than 12–14 days from San Francisco to Washington. During the winter, shipping was the only freight means on a route by way of South America, and it took 4 months before it arrived. The American author, Brad English is of the opinion that a bet was the reason for Jon taking on the mail route, and Stein Eriksen wrote in his book that he was to get two

To the left
The Olympic flame has been lit twice from the hearth of Øverbø in Morgedal. In 1952 it came to Oslo by ski relay, and in 1960 by car to Oslo and plane to the USA in Squaw Valley. In Morgedal they are now waiting to hear whether the Olympic Games in 1992 will be held at Lillehammer. In that case the fire will be lit again in the hearth at Morgedal.

Top right
Postcart from Duluth.

Bottom right
Carl Hovelsen was a great attraction in the circus in the USA. This plaque has been very kindly lent to us from the Circus World Museum, Baraboo, Wisconsin. Hovelsen later returned to Norway and took part in the Holmenkollen competition in 1926 and 1927, at the age of 50 years. He received the Holmenkollen Medal as early as 1903.

No. 704
Ames-Huntley Co., Duluth
INTERNATIONAL WINTER SPORT. A 100 Foot Jump on Skis.

THE BARNUM & BAILEY
GREATEST
SHOW ON EARTH
CAPT. CARL HOWELSEN
THE PERILOUS SCANDINAVIAN WINTER SPORT
IN ALL ITS WILD AND WONDROUS DARING
SKI SAILING
FRIGHTFUL FALCON FLIGHTS ON SKIMMING SKEES
BY CAPT. CARL HOWELSEN,
WHO AT A SINGLE BOUND COVERS A DISTANCE OF OVER SEVENTY FIVE FEET AND SPANS A YAWNING, DEATH-INVITING CHASM. AN ACT OF A THOUSAND THRILLS, SEEN FOR THE FIRST TIME THIS SIDE OF NORWAYS SNOW-CAPPED PEAKS.

Snowshoe Thompson is still the great ski-pioneer in the USA. His skiing feats are vividly depicted in both the history books and the comic strips.

hundred dollars a month no matter how deep the snow was. «Snowshoes» were what the Americans called skis, and Jon got the nickname «Snowshoe Thompson» when he set out. For a couple of years someone had tried to keep up the route on Indian snowshoes, but the snow was too deep and he had to give up. The year was 1856 and the postbag weighed around 20 kg. His skis were from a Telemark model and they were 2.70 m long. Jon had made them himself from memory. The mail route went from Placerville in California to Carson Valley in Nevada, and was about 130 km each way through wild mountain terrain. Whether it was a bet or not, it certainly lasted. For 20 years Jon maintained the dramatic mountain route, in all kinds of weather and with all kinds of snow conditions. He used around three days on the trip. With time several other mail routes by ski or snowshoes became established, and the ski historian, Bill Berry of the «U.S. Ski Association and National Ski Hall of Fame» writes as follows:

«Skis, first known as snowshoes, were necessary resources in the early winters of the gold-rush period. They were introduced by Norwegians, and the use of the long boards spread quickly. Around 1860 skis played a leading role in the conquering of the American West.»

Snowshoe Thompson died only 49 years old. Even today American ski historians write that his records are hard to beat. And those who have worked hardest to spread the Telemark style during the last ten years, held up Jon Tosteinsen as the great ideal. «His success shows that courage, daring, faith in oneself and good training on skis are the best qualities a good skier requires.

Norwegians organized skiing

In the Eastern states and in the Midwest skiing spread with the Norwegian emigrants who left the old country between 1875 and 1895. And there were many of them – over 260,000! Among these were some of the elite skiers from Telemark, those who had both started competition skiing and made skis popular in outdoor life in their home country. Sondre Norheim settled with his wife and seven children in North-Dakota in 1894. Mikkel Hemmestveit came to Minnesota in 1888 and his brother Torjus followed him in 1889. Others from Telemark settled in Wisconsin and Michigan.

In the 1880's Norwegian skiclubs grew up all over the Eastern states and the Midwest.

In 1882, Carl Illstrup from Drammen hastened the organization of the Minneapolis Ski Club, and in a short time there were clubs all over Minnesota and Wisconsin. Each club had its own «uniform» and almost only Norwegians among its members. Members in the Red Wing Club had blue ski pants, jacket and cap, and on the cap and jacket was a decorative border of imitation gold. All speeches were given in Norwegian and Norwegian ski songs were sung.

In 1883 came «The Nansen Ski-Club of Berlin, New Hampshire» and with that ski sport was organized that far east as well. Here there was more fun and games attached to the university milieu, and the club was named after the great folk hero, Fridtjof Nansen. On January 14, 1888, there was a ski competition at Eau Claire, in Wisconsin. Over 6,000 spectators aplauded the daring jumpers with delight and enthusiasm. They had never seen anything like it before. Both the organized ski clubs and these ski competitions were very important. They gave the new settlers from Norway a feeling of belonging, and they extended the skiing tradition from their home country. Torjus Hemmestveit wrote home to the ski club in Kristiania and put it this way: «The roots of skiing came from Morgedal. We from Telemark took a branch of it and planted it in America where it now grows and thrives.»

It wasn't just those from Telemark who took their skis with them to the USA. They were in the majority in Minnesota, but other states were dominated by emigrants from Trøndelag or the north of Norway. The American Ski Association was established at Ishpeming on Lake Superior. There, there were mainly people from Trøndelag and one of them was Karl Tellefsen. In this mining-town of Ishpeming, one of the first jumping hills in America was built. Later it was extended with an

Karl Tellefsen from Trondheim became the first president of the American Ski Association.

NIAGARA IN AN EMPTY BARREL

«This winter we read about a Norwegian who in a public competition abroad showed so little sense that he amused the spectators by soaring out from the jump on one ski.

Skiing should be kept free of sensational circus feats. Those who demand breakneck and nerve-shattering events should travel to America and watch some daredevil go down the Niagara Falls in an empty barrel!»
(Fritz Huitfeldt: Skiløbning i text og billeder 1908)

artificial scaffolding, and got the name «suicide hill» because it looked so frightening. On this hill a jumping competition was arranged every year on George Washington's birthday. After the jumping competition on Februar 22, 1904, a group of enthusiastic Norwegian ski leaders and an American journalist came together and founded «The National Ski Association of America». Karl Tellefsen was the first president of the organization, and thereby the foundation was laid for one of the greatest organizations on the American continent. They stuck to their Nowegian traditions, both in customs and expressions from the old country, and this has undoubtedly contributed to the fact that norwegian ski expressions are still alive all over the world.

Where were those from Telemark in the midst of all this development? Mikkel Hemmestveit from Morgedal, who among other things ran the first ski school in the world in Kristiania, made his living mainly from his knowledge about skiing in America. In 1881 he established a world record in jumping at Red Wing. He jumped then 102 feet, which in meters would be a jump of over 31 meters. This record stood for 6 years until Svein Sollid jumped 31.5 m in Morgedal in 1897. Mikkel Hemmestveit lived in St. Croix Falls in Minnesota, where he earned money by making skis which he got another Norwegian to help him to sell. Ski historians are nevertheless of the opinion that it was Aksel Holter in Ashland, Michigan who did the most to spread Norwegian skis throughout the USA at the turn of the century. He made Telemark skis from Sondre Norheim's model, and the harnesses were a copy of the prize-winning Huitfeldt bindings. His ski factory made thousands of pairs of skis, and he was himself secretary in the American Ski Association. Ashland Working, as his factory was called, had 20 employees and distributed skis after the Telemark model all over the Midwest. In November, 1905, a group of 28 Norwegians came together and formed the «NORGE Ski Club of Chicago». During the subsequent 10-year period, this club came to be the nucleus of skiing in Midwest. The club arranged ski competitions with up to 30,000 spectators, and the club is just as active today as it was then.

The American west had preliminarily very little to do with skiing. Another Norwegian was to play an important role in skiing out there. Karl Hovelsen was born in Christiania in 1877, and he emigrated to Chicago in 1905. In 1903 he was awarded both Kongepokalen (the King's

To the right
In the winter of 1986 Sun Valley and Ski Magazine celebrated their anniversary as if it were the ski anniversary for the whole of the USA. Perhaps they should rather have celebrated the 150th anniversary of the Nattestad brothers who brought skis to the USA in 1836?

America's
50TH
Ski Birthday
50 YEARS AND GOLDEN!
1986 is Golden Anniversary year for Sun Valley and Ski Magazine. Celebrate with us the skiing birthday party of the century in Sun Valley, Idaho on February 1-7, 1986. For more information and reservations for this week and other golden anniversary activities throughout the season, please write Sun Valley Company, Sun Valley, Idaho 83353 or call 1-800-635-8261.
Sun Valley
GOLDEN ANNIVERSARY
SKI

3178
1366
166
2455
1347
1080
3185
1746
2279
3485
2398
3513
1309
1646
253

Cup) and the Holmenkollen Medal. The way in which he made himself a pioneer of skiing in the USA was hardly in accordance with the characteristic Telemark style. He took a job as «The Daring Young Man in the Circus», and the huge, well-known Barnum and Bailey Circus built an enormous jumping hill in the ring of the circus. This «Greatest Show on Earth» attracted in 1907 nearly 4 million spectators, who stared with open mouths while Hovelsen jumped on skis on the artificial hill. When the «Flying Norwegian» settled in Colorado in 1909, he suddenly realized how much skiing enjoyment one could have in this mountainous part of America. It became an important goal for him to make other Americans aware of how valuable outdoor skiing could be for everyone. Hovelsen built ski hills in many cities and invited other skiers from the Midwest and the Eastern states to come and compete with him. People came by the thousands to watch these competitions, and interest was so great that the first ski clubs were organized. Both young and old started to ski, and Hovelsen travelled around in Colorado and gave instruction to enthusiastic

Top left
For 15 years the American Birkebeiner Race has gathered thousands of skiers to Telemark Lodge in Wisconsin. This is called skiing's answer to the Boston Marathon.

Together with his brother Lars, Anders Haugen from Bø in Telemark sought his fortune in America. He is the jumper who has achieved the best result for the USA in the Winter Olympics. In the municipality centre in Bø are to be found some of the prizes he won. In his later years he travelled around the USA making publicity for skiing by jumping on artificial hills which looked quite frightening. Here he is jumping at a stadium in Los Angeles at the age of 60.

Americans. 50-60 years later it was in the same state of Colorado that active ski-instructors took up the Telemark style in skiing and created a renaissance of the classical Telemark way of skiing.

Around 1915 there were better ski jumpers in the USA than in Norway. Ragnar Omtvedt from Chicago set a world record in jumping in 1916 of 58.5 m in Steamboat Springs in Colorado, and the ski hill was known as Carl Hovelsen Hill. Two years later, Henry Hall from Michigan beat him by 10 feet, and this record held for two more years. Then along came Anders Haugen from Minnesota, originally from Bø in Telemark, with a jump of almost 65 m. His brother, Lars, also from Minnesota, and Carl Hovelsen jumped around 60 m, and this was much farther than jumpers in Europe were doing at that time. These world records in Colorado contributed a great deal to the self-confidence of the American ski-jumpers.

At the Olympic Games in 1924, Anders Haugen was awarded a bronze medal in the jumping competition. This is USA's best placing up to today. The one who has been closest is Jeff Hastings who came 4th at the Olympic Games in Sarajevo in 1984. And now it is Hastings, together with Bill Koch and Craig Ward who will set the pace in the TIMEX Skiathlom in the USA.

The ski pioneers from Norway brought with them unusual expertise to the new world. They gave young and old Americans an interest in skiing both for competition and recreation. Today there are more than 13 million skiers in the USA. However, there aren't many of them who know that skiing came from Norway.

AUSTRIA AND ALPINE SKIING

The alpine technique which had developed in Central Europe up to 1920, was widely advertised and became very popular in the USA. Alpine skiing had very high status, and with the opening of the Sun Valley centre in 1936, skiing had engaged the American jet set. American stars knew very little about skiing's roots in Telemark, and even less about the origin of «slalom», skis, and the «Telemark and Kristiania Technique». It was most ski instructors from Austria who introduced alpine skiing to the USA. Felix Schaffgotsch was given the responsibility of finding a good place for alpine skiing. The only condition demanded of the Austrian by Averell Harriman, who had commissioned him, was that he should find an area which resembled the best ski centres in Austria and Switzerland. And far up in the mountains in Idaho they found the place which was to become USA's leading ski-centre, «America's St. Moritz», Sun Valley. Few people realized that Sigmund Ruud was the advisor for the building of the first jumping hill in Sun Valley.

In 1938, Sigmund and Birger Ruud were in Sun Valley. Sigmund wrote concerning this visit: «The Austrians have been very smart with their ski schools. Their propaganda has been very cleverly organized, yes, so cleverly that the majority of Americans have a lot to say about skiing in the Alps and these famous alpine resorts, but what they know about Norway is practically nothing.

Today, circumstances are such that non-Norwegians have forgotten or have never learned that it was the Norwegians who introduced skiing to central Europe and the rest of the world.

Norwegian ski-pioneers

Reports of Fridtjof Nansen's incredible trip across Greenland were exciting reading for young people in Central Europe. Special interest was attached to the use of skis on the Greenland expedition and was an inspiration to outdoor sports enthusiasts. Could these wooden boards also be used on steep Alpine slopes? In Austria there were two Norwegians who for the first time demonstrated the effective use of skis. Masterbaker Samson from Kristiania was to complete his training i Vienna, and at the Norwegian-Swedish consulate, Georg Wedel Jarlsberg was working. The snow

Top left
The Sun Valley centre was modelled after similar centres in Central Euorpe. However, there is still a Ruud hill christened after Sigmund Ruud who helped create the jumping hill. The idea behind Sun Valley came from the chairman of the board for the Union Pacific Railroad, Averell Harriman, who wanted to find a winter resort for passengers on the luxury train.

Middle left
Sun Valley was the place where the American stars romped on the ski hills. Louis Armstrong preferred to stay on the level.

Bottom left
The first stamp in the world with a ski motif was issued in Hungary, showing a skier in the Telemark style.

came early in the atumn of 1892, and the two of them took out their skis and impressed people who had never seen skiing before. Samson jumped 8–10 meters on a hill of manure, and everyone cheered.

«In the Autumn of 1892, baron Wedel Jarlsberg gave a lecture at the Agricultural Society, on skiing, and this made a deep impression. He described in glowing words the inimitable pleasure it was to ski on these swift boards and he showed pictures and instructive drawings and gave excellent information.

This lecture gave the impulse toward the formation of the «Niederösterreichischer Ski-Verein» on the 8th of November, 1892.»

Thus wrote Felix Schmal concerning the start of skiing in Austria. Other newspaper articles and literary sources were of the opinion that these Norwegians really were the pioneers who first gave the stimulus to the enormous interest in skiing which developed in the coming years. They gave skiing instruction and already during the

«OPEN-AIR RECREATION IS UPROOTED»

«The turn which Nansen and his comrades called the «telemarksving» is now sold in plastic wrapping as a «telemarking» – «Made in USA». Life in the open air, which should have given us an opportunity for mingled impressions of nature in a world full of restless changes, is also uprooted.»
(Nils Faarlund in «Snø og Ski» No. 1/85)

winter of 1893 they had over 100 pairs of skis sent down from Norway. Jacob Vaage, the ski historian, has recorded valuable conversations with these ski pioneers, and Samson has given a vivid account of the first skiiing competiton in Austria, February 3, 1893. There were few participants in this meet, but Samson impressed everyone.

«My skis were made by Evensen, a wheelwright from Slependen, and the spectators evidently thought that my speed on them was terrific. They asked me to jump as well, and I had a jumping hill made and flew like a bird through the air. At any rate that is what the spectators said when they told others about it later. They swung their hats, shouted and cried out, and they beamed when I landed down on the outrun after the jump. I waved back again. It was a great day.»

The following year the Austrians sent an invitation to one of the best skiers in Norway. By now there were so many skilled skiers around Kristiania that it wasn't necessary to go as far as Telemark to find worthy representatives for Norwegian skiing. Jonas Holmen was sent down and other Norwegians who were studying and

Nansen's trip across Greenland created publicity for skiing and aroused interest over the whole world.

working in Central Europe also participated in the competition down there. They won all the prizes in both jumping and downhill and finally in cross-country. This was the competition for the first Austrian championship and for the «Alperosen» trophy. Holmen started last and overtook the one after the other, and finally a small, squarely built Austrian. We will let Holmen tell the rest himself, as he told it to Jacob Vaage. «Soon, we overtook him too. And then there was just the downhill left, and it was an easy matter to beat them all. They weren't much good at downhill. When I reached the goal, there was no one to be seen at the time-keepers' table. Those in charge were all in the inn drinking beer and enjoying themselves. When someone called out that one of the Norwegians had come in, the one who had started last, you should have seen them come flying out. They rushed out with stopwatches in their hands, and they must have been adept timekeepers, for they timed me down to a tenth of a second: 55,53,6.»

The first «Alperose» trophy therefore went to Holmen. At a later date, Karl and Eyvind Roll went to Austria and competed with the other Norwegians Gustav Thaulow, Karl Sondresen and T. Mønniche. Twenty years later, the Austrian Ski Association made a yearbook which marked twenty years of skiing. In this yearbook, Felix Schmel wrote as follows about the competition in 1895: «One of the Norwegians decided that he would make a trial jump. This happened very quickly and to everyone's surprise. He soared through the air, then down to the snow and right into the midst of the crowd of people, or so it appeared! However, the aghast spectators had no cause for fear: At the last second he made an abrupt turn and calmly came to a halt, looking straight ahead as if nothing had happened.» Once again the «Alperose» went to Norway and publicity about skiing kept on increasing. After the skiing competitons that year, over 500 pairs of skis were sold in Vienna.

In 1897 another championship was held. This time it was Yngvar Knudtzon from Trondheim who won. Taking into account their performance on the jumping hills in recent years, it can be clearly seen that the Austrians certainly knew how to carry on the Norwegian ski traditions. In recognition of their contribution as ski pioneers in Austria, Wedel Jarlsberg, Samson and Fridtjof Nansen were made honorary presidents of the Austrian Ski Association.

In Austria Zdarsky is considered the father of alpine skiing. He used one pole and short skis in the Alpine terrain (see below).

SAFE IN THE TELEMARK POSITION

«In snow conditions like this, it is safest to run in the Telemark position. I remember once I was a few thousand feet above Meiringen in dense snow, and darkness was falling. We had crossed up Faulhorn and climbed to a height of 8,000 feet that day. We skied down to 1500 feet with wretched visibility, in this Telemark position. The strange thing was that even when the snow conditions changed abruptly, we managed without a fall.»
(Sir Arnold Lunn: Alpine skiing 1921)

The controversy with Mathias Zdarsky

Just before the turn of the century, an odd fellow turned up from Lillienfeld in Austria. He made his own skis, made propaganda for his own skiing technique in Alpine terrain and made derogatory remarks about everything that had to do with Norwegian skiing traditions. His name was Mathias Zdarsky, and he criticized everything from Norwegian skiboots to bindings, skis and technique. He called Norwegian ski technique primitive nonsense. There was a terrific upropar. Norwegian skiing had won many friends in

Europe and they called our skiing «the Norwegian school».These friends joined in the fight against «the Lillienfeld skiing», and strong words were used on both sides.

Both the technique, skis and bindings Zdarsky used were strange to us Norwegians. He used one pole on which he rode down the slopes of the valleys, and when his speed became too great, he threw himself to the side in the snow. Zdarsky's skis were much shorter than the Norwegian skis. Compared with the wild runs in Morgedal, the Zdarsky style was careful, hesitant and slow. Jakob Vaage recounts that his skis had a peculiar braking apparatus which was exhibited in Ludvig Torgersen's sports shop – where it was used rather as an effective mousetrap.

Nonetheless, Zdarsky's ideas contributed a great deal to alpine skiing on steep slopes. In 1897 he wrote a book which many consider to be the basis of modern alpine skiing. In our own Ski Association's yearbook of 1905, Hasse Horn wrote «Zdarsky has always been a very useful man for the alpinists.» However, Norwegian skiing ideas were not completely forgotten. «I believe that the alpinists in con-

The Arlberg region in Austria has developed into a skiing Mecca, with hundreds of lifts and well-prepared hills.

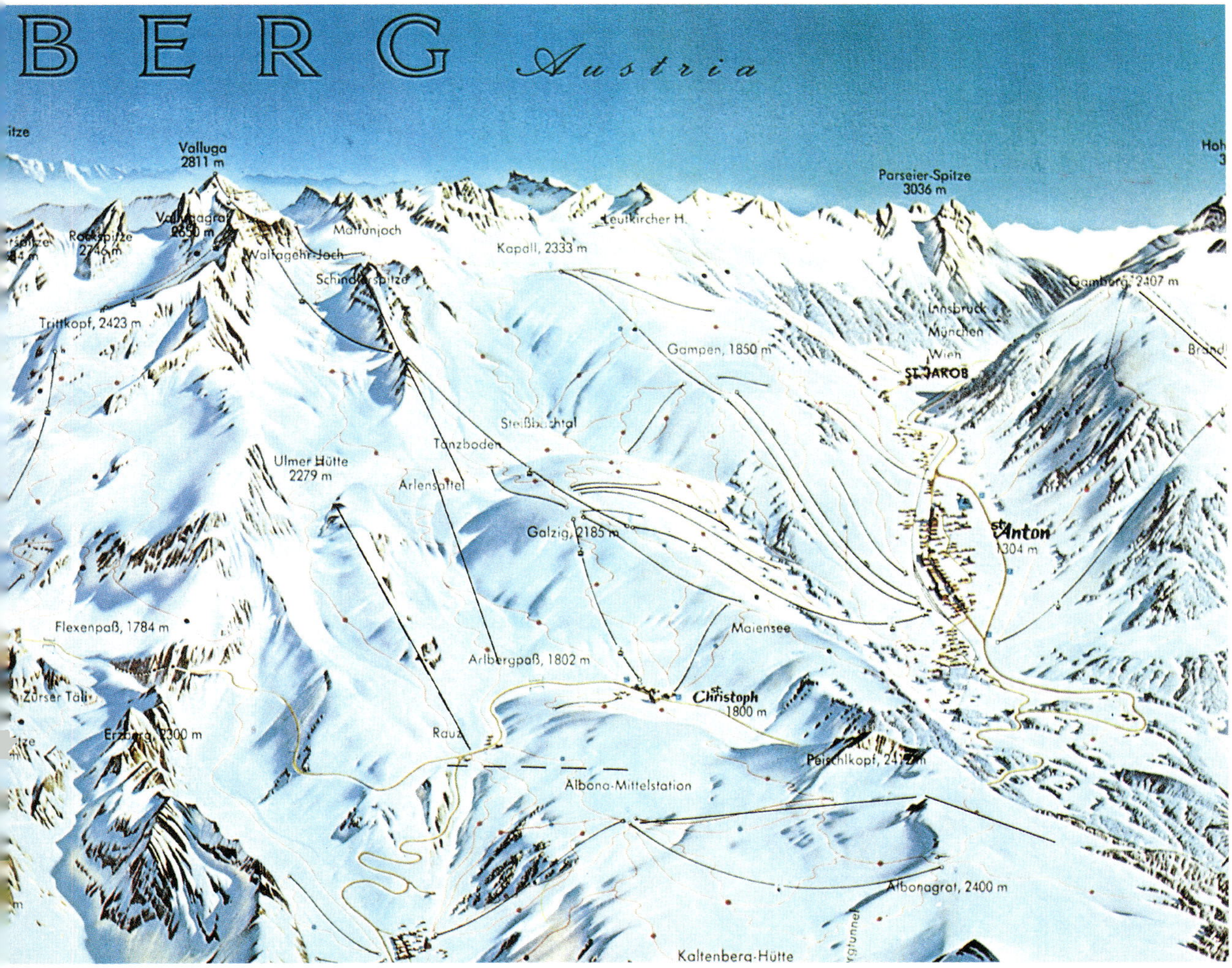

HOPSCOTCH JUMPING

«The most recent form of slalom has also deviated. Originally it was a run with fluid movement in the turns. Now the slalåm gates are placed in such a way that it has all become too chopped up and unnatural. It has become a game of «hopscotch».»
(Sigmund Ruud, 1938)

junction with us, came themselves to the conclusion that their attitude has been somewhat one-sided. They have obviously concentrated totally on the steep precipices and as a result of this, neglected to develop the all-around dexterity that we demand of a skier. However, this can gradually be corrected, and here we Norwegians can make our contribution, as long as we can approach the alpinists with understanding. Quite possibly we could both benefit from cooperation.»

However, the controversy with Zdarsky kept on for many years. Several years later he wrote in an American ski magazine that the Norwegians had stolen the ski sport from Finland. Fortunately other skiers were more serious.

The Arlberg School, Lunn and modern alpinism

The Arlberg Pass in Austria was an important traffic artery for mail and goods to Switzerland right up to the turn of the century. In St. Anton and Stuben they had their own Post Hotel, and there had been a flourishing traffic. However, between 1895 and 1900, much of this traffic went over the Flexen Pass, and then the skiers took over the guest beds at Arlberg. Many of them who had read Nansen in bed, or who had gone to Samson's or Wedel Jarlsberg's or Zdarsky's ski school, went up to the Arlberg area to try out their skiing. In particular they went to Hospitz in St. Christoph, 1771 m above sealevel. From there it was a fair trip up to Mainsee and Galzig, 2181 m.a.s.l. The run down from there to St. Anton which lay at about 1300 m.a.s.l. was a thrill, even with the equipment in use around the year 1900. For this terrain was something quite different from the «hair-raising runs» in Morgedal in Telemark. Here are precipitous Alpine mountainsides with few rounded hills or spruce-clad slopes. Another technique was necessary. Viktor Sohn founded the Arlberg Ski Club in 1901. This was the start of a development toward modern alpinism as we know it today. From Arlberg we see the start of specialization, with separate skis for alpine skiing.

In 1906, Sohn organized the first ski courses in the Arlberg area. The course took place in the little district of Zürs, not far from Lech, and among the pupils was 16 year-old Hannes Schneider. The year after, he was a ski instructor at a hotel in St. Anton, and he was the one who in 1922 founded the world renowned Arlberg Ski School. In this year, also, the pre-

To the right
A Telemark skier in the Alps in 1907 and an alpine trail in Telemark in 1940. The motif above is from Boval Lodge with the Morteratschgletscher glacier. The planned Gausta Course (below) was a fantastic run, but the war stopped the World Championships in 1940. Active skiing enthusiasts in Rjukan are now working to construct a new run where the old one became overgrown during the war years. The plan is for Rjukan at last to be placed on the world map as an alpine centre in Northern Europe.

1883 m. o. h.
6,5 km
3,5 km. Svineroe
1019 m. o. h
550 m. o. h.
DALE
240 m.

sident of the British Ski Association, Sir Arthur Lunn, proposed his pioneering rules for marking and setting up slalom-runs. The novelty was that the runs should have gates, or control marking as they called it. Judging of style was removed and technique was made optional. The various Kristiania turns were more and more used, and gradually the «parallel» technique took over in all competitions and runs. In München, in 1922, there was also arranged a competition in the Telemark combination, cross-country, jumping and slalom.

Mürren, in Switzerland had had ski competitions since 1903. A duke who took a skiing holiday there every year, donated in 1911 a valuable cup as the main trophy for the competition. This duke came from India and was known as Duke Robert of Kandhar, and he gave his name to the competitions which later became so famous. The active Hannes Schneider from Arlberg persuaded Arnold Lunn to go

Top left
The monks in the St. Bernard monastery reputedly first saw a Norwegian on skis, and started to ski themselves.

Bottom left
In the Jura mountains at the border between France and Switzerland, this Telemark skier figured on a poster in 1912.

Above right
Here in the mountains above Zürs were held the first ski courses in Austria. Today, skiers from the whole world flock here. The Arlberg region has skiing conditions from early in the winter until far into the spring, and quite exceptional service facilities.

Below to the right
This style has been predominant in many alpine centres.

ZÜRS
12
17

«THE SONS OF OLD TELEMARK»

«Slalom comes from Telemark. Skiers from Telemark were our first skiing teachers, that we all know. They were the ones who could ski down a hill so that their tracks formed continuous, snaking curves. The sons of old Telemark were the ones to perform the first ski-jumps and the most able to make their way in the terrain. If anybody should be thanked because the sport of skiing so rapidly became popular and grew to be the national sport of Norway it must be the skiers from Telemark.»
(Sigmund Ruud: Skispor krysser verden, Oslo 1938)

TRICKY TRIVIA

Q.8. He is considered the father of modern skiing:
A. MATHIAS ZDARSKY
B. SONDRE NORHEIM
C. HANNES SCHNEIDER
D. CHARLES PROCTOR
ANSWER: In 1860, Sondre Norheim, a resident of Telemark, Norway, jumped farther than any other skier of the turning tracks downhill («sla-lom» for «sloping track» in Telemark dialect) and fashioned a stiff toe-and-heel binding for greater control, bringing skiing into the modern age.»
(Questions and answers in the anniversary issue SKI Collectors Edition 1986)

with him in arranging the competiton in St. Anton every other year. Now, this honoured traditional competition is held alternately at St. Anton in Austria, Garmisch-Partenkirchen in West Germany, Chamonix in France, Sestrière in Italy, and of course at Mürren in Switzerland.

«For slalom and downhill skiing, this competition plays the same role as our Holmenkollen competition. It is the most splendid competition of its kind. Just after the Kandahar Club had been started, the Swiss Academic Ski Club was founded. The main purpose of this club was also to work for the promotion of slalom and downhill sport. From then on things began to move quickly, and clubs with the same purpose turned up also in the other Alpine countries. All these worked enthusiastically for the new forms of competitions which caught on quickly in Central Europe. In 1928, such progress had been made that Arnold Lunn proposed that slalom and downhill should be incorporated into the International Ski Association's competition program, thereby placing them on an equal level with jumping and cross-country skiing. This, however, the ski congress would not agree to at the time. It was decided that the interested federations should experiment and arrange competitions of this kind on a trial basis.

The year after, during the World Championships in Zakopane, downhill and slalom were included as trial competitions. At the international ski congress in Oslo and at Finse in 1930, these new disciplines were given official recognition. And then the rules for slalom and downhill were approved by the F.I.S. The rules had already been tried out at competitions in Trondheim and at Rjukan in 1929.»

Sigmund Ruud who wrote this, should together with others of our skiers be given the main credit for bringing Alpine skiing and slalom back to Norway. They went to Central Europe to compete in ski-jumping, but took part in slalom and downhill competitions just for the fun of it. They participated in alpine competitions one day, and jumping the next day. Sigmund Ruud

Hannes Schneider, creator of the new style and the Arlberg system.

fought tooth and nail against a development of closely placed gates in the slalomhill. «This would ruin the sport,» was his opinion. «I maintain that slalom is not a sport for adult skiers, but excellent for women and children.»

The first ski-tow was opened at Tryvannskleiva in 1937, and on that same hill they acquired electric time-keeping in 1940. That year, the Gausta run at Rjukan in Telemark was ready to receive the World Championships in downhill, but the war put a stop to their plans. The Gausta run was one of the toughest in the world, and active ski enthusiasts in Rjukan are working now to put this international run in order. It has a drop of 1,000 m and resembles «Streif», the Hahnenkamm run in Kitzbühl.

The enthusiastic Ruud brothers, Sigmund, Birger and Asbjørn, were the last skiers in the genuine Telemark tradition. When Birger Ruud became Olympic champion in both downhill and jumping in 1936, he marked the end of a ski era.

Hannes Schneider Born in Austria in 1890, died in the USA in 1955.

Even today there are Norwegians who refuse to accept the term «alpinism» to denote the events slalom, giant slalom and downhill, or for skiing in steep mountain terrain. They are of the opinion that the old Norwegian names are good enough. They quite ignore the fact that it was in the Alps that slalom from Morgedal developed into one of the most popular ski disciplines.

«. . . . a blond, blue-eyed young man with «sex appeal» who dashed out into the world in 1952 . . .»

«THEY MUST BE MAD»

«At the Christiania Skiklub's first competition on the Huseby hill in 1879, the Danish prince Hans was one of the spectators. When the first man from Telemark soared out from the jump with a little branch in one hand while he took off his cap with the other it is said that the prince exclaimed: «Dammit, this can't be true! They must be mad!»
(From the Ski Association's 50-Year Anniversary book, 1933)

Towards the mid-twenties popular ski centres grew up in Central Europe. Skiing opened the way for winter tourism, and the hotels advertised good skiing conditions.

The most outstanding creator of the new style was Hannes Schneider from Zürs in Arlberg, Austria. He started as ski instructor at a hotel in the Arlberg area in 1907, and gradually formed his own technique with emphasis on strong rotation to press through a turn on steep slopes.

Together with the Englishman, Arnold Lunn, he created a system for competitions, and he instructed pupils who later were to go to the USA and promote «Alpinism» there. Otto Lang, Friedl Pfeifer and Sepp Rusch took along with them Schneider's Arlberg system to the American ski centres, and dominated skiing in the USA during the thirties. When Sigmund Ruud complained in 1938 that the Austrians had taken over all skiing, it was Schneider's Arlberg School he meant.

When Hitler annexed Austria in 1938, all the ski schools were closed and Schneider was arrested. He was let out after a year and left for the USA, where he started a ski school in North Conway.

The Arlberg Ski School in Austria is today the leading ski school in slalom and alpine skiing. «First control, then speed» was Schneider's slogan in good Mathias Zdarsky tradition. Schneider strongly emphasized weight distribution in the turning phase; hence technically, it is here that the lasting value of Schneider's work lies. However, we shall not forget that all the time it was the parallel turn from Morgedal, the Kristiania turn, that he embroidered on, and made into alpine ski technique.

To the right
The Olympic Games in Oslo in 1952 were a large and demanding arrangement for a country in the middel of reconstruction after the war. But the Games increased our self-confidence, through the good results and the well organized arrangement.

VI OLYMPIC WINTER GAMES
14.-25. FEBRUARY OSLO NORWAY 1952

NORGES
SKIFORBUND
ÅRBOK 1954

Stein Eriksen

After the war alpine skiing changed in various ways. To begin with, all alpine skiing had more and more been centred on Central Europe. One had to be from the Alps to be the best in the world. This was a developement that had to end. Secondly, it was important to get money and professional status for alpine skiing on a line with other ski sports. The third change was the introduction of freestyle, and the requirement that skiing should not only be judged against a stopwatch, but also according to style and elegance.

It is worthwhile to note that it was a single skier who set in motion these changes. «They were incorporated in a blond, blue-eyed young man with «sex appeal» who dashed out into the world in 1952,» wrote the American magazine SKI. During the winter Olympics in Oslo, Stein Eriksen danced down between flags and gates to a gold and a silver medal. After that he strengthened his position as a great skier by taking two gold medals in slalom, giant slalom and triple combination in the World Championships two years later.

Stein Eriksen then went to the USA and did what no one before him had done: He made money out of his popularity and skill as a skier. When the ski centres begged him to come, Stein travelled from ski school to ski school and doubled his fee each time. He travelled from Boyne to Heavenly Valley, from there to Aspen, Sugarbush and back to the Rocky Mountains. Ski producers paid for using his name on their products, and he opened his own ski shop. He obtained exclusive contracts with magazines and television, and he imported his own ski clothes. Stein Eriksen's skill in making money became a model for skiers and agents for many years to come.

What made this possible was a ski style which was so superior and dancing that it pepped up a whole nation. At the end of the fifties, there was only one slogan to be heard in ski centres all over the USA: «Ski like Stein», and the girls . . .

He skied with his feet glued together, while the upper part of his body formed what looked like a large comma, but which even more gave the impression that he defied the laws of physics. It was a delight to watch. Millions of Americans saw Stein's fantastic turns over and over again in magazines, in films and on television.

Much of Stein Eriksen's ski style was based on gymnastics and play in his youth, in the same way as with the Ruud brothers in Kongsberg. Therefore he has continued all the time to turn somersaults on skis, and in this manner opened the way for the new freestyle sports which now also have reached Norway. More than anything else it is his way of making skiing attractive to watch which has caused freestyle and ballet skiing to develop as they have during the last 30 years. When one picture in his book was instrumental in releasing the new Telemark renaissance, it emphasizes the enormous influence Stein Eriksen has and has had on all-round American skiing.

To the left
The Ruud brothers from Kongsberg were the first Norwegians to do well in alpine competitions in Central Europe. They took the sport back home with them, but it was first with Stein Eriksen that this branch of skiing received its well-deserved impetus. When he won the World Championships at Åre in 1954 he was pictured on the front page of the Norwegian Ski Federation's Yearbook. Up until then this front page had been dominated by cross-country skiing and jumping.

TIMEX SKIATHLOM

Idea and Background

In the spring of 1981, a strange ski competition was arranged at the Trak Telemark Camp at Mazama, Washington. It was called the «Berzerkebeinerrennet» – a mixture of Birkebeiner and berserk! The competition was a reaction against the specialized slalom competitions for Telemark skiers, where the equipment now more and more came to resemble the alpine. The Berzerkebeinerrennet in 1981 was a kind of forerunner of the TIMEX Skiathlom, even if Fred Olsen has never heard of it. As the illustration shows, the jumping contest from the old Telemark combination is lacking, but Eric Sanford who projected the run, wanted it to be a proper mountain trip in miniature. The woods and the terrain should decide the profile of the run, and it should demand an all-round use for cross-country skis.

The author and ski journalist, Steve Barnett, was one of the front figures within the Telemark revolution in the USA. In October, 1981, he brought the development during the last ten years into focus in an article in the Cross Country ski Magazine: «The Telemark Revolution: It's Gone Too Far». He wrote in the article that both the equipment and the ski competitions have developed far away from the ideas which came from Morgedal 100 years earlier, and from Colorado early in the seventies. Equipment consisting of high boots and skintight ski suits was unsuitable for skiing freely cross-country, was his opinion, and the Telemark competitions on prepared slalom hills were more alpinism than skiing in the Telemark tradition. «What is really necessary is another arrangement, which is not so strictly regulated, which accepts Nordic skiing on its own premises. Since Telemark equipment can be used in all directions, then the ideal ski competition should go in all directions. The gates must not be limited to combinations which are best suited for slalom skis. A natural Telemark slalom should have hills to climb with traversed gates as well as gates for downhill. Telemark slalom competitions in the future should be more like a real run through the woods - with a rapid descent down through the trees, fast poling up the hills, over obstacles, long strides across extensive flat terrain, and hard climbing through dense woods. The participants can choose for themselves what technique they want to use at the different stages in the run.»

«AND THEN SKIING BECAME FASHIONABLE»

«The Telemark skiers really got things moving, and we stared and our eyes bulged, when one of these marvels soared out from the jump – without poles. That they could take the impact on their legs alone, we failed to understand. However, as we had inherited a certain imitative ability we naturally stumbled after them, and thus skiing became fashionable. (Fritz Huitfeldt: Skiløbning i text og billeder 1908)

These suggestions of Steve Barnett's are in accordance with good Telemark tradition, but they didn't gain much support in the USA.

In Norway the idea was proposed again, even though in another form, five years later. Fred Olsen presented his idea for a TIMEX Skiathlom at a press conference November 11, 1985, and this was almost 100 years since the Hemmestveits had participated in a corresponding competition in Seljord in 1886. In keeping with the best ski traditions from Telemark, the ski-enthusiastic shipowner presented a varied competition plan for increased enjoyment of skiing on one pair of skis. The skiathlom idea was worked out by him together with ski-interested family members at the end of the 1985 ski season. Ivar Formo was contacted as consultant, and it was he who drafted the idea further with the Norwegian Ski Association and Marc Hodler in FIS. Fred Olsen connected the idea with TIMEX, and spred the idea throughout the world in the autumn of 1985.

It is the Norwegian Ski Association which has contributed toward the development of a simple set of regulations for the TIMEX Skiathlom, and together with the Åsnes Ski Factory, a great deal of planning has been done to find a suitable ski model for these ski competitions. The idea was to go back to the original skiing, as they arranged it in Telemark in the previous century. Therefore it was given the name, the Telemark combination, – slalom skiing, jumping on several small hills, and cross-country skiing in a small loop between the jumping hill and the slalom hill.

The first competition was arranged in Vrådal in Telemark, the 5th of January, 1986. Vrådal is in the Kviteseid municipality, on the other side of the valley to Morgedal – the cradle of skiing. From the same municipality as Sondre Norheim's ski trails went out from, the «Skiathlom» now went out to the world. Over 13,000 were in the competition in Norway the first winter. In the USA probably about 40,000 competed. In Norway it concluded with the Skarve competition at Geilo, the 25th of April. Here the entire Norwegian ski team participated, and the Åsnes Ski Factory presented there the first specially made all-round skis for the Skiathlom.

What separates Barnett's idea and Fred Olsen's Skiathlom is the slalom and that Barnett's combination lacks the jumping. Steve Barnett wanted the course preferably to go through free, unprepared terrain, as similar as possible to natural wooded country, so that the skier could really show his skill. In the Timex Skiathlom the first winter, one alternately started and finished with jumping. Most of the competitions have taken place at different ski centres, but they can easily be arranged in any open country or at a mountain cabin.

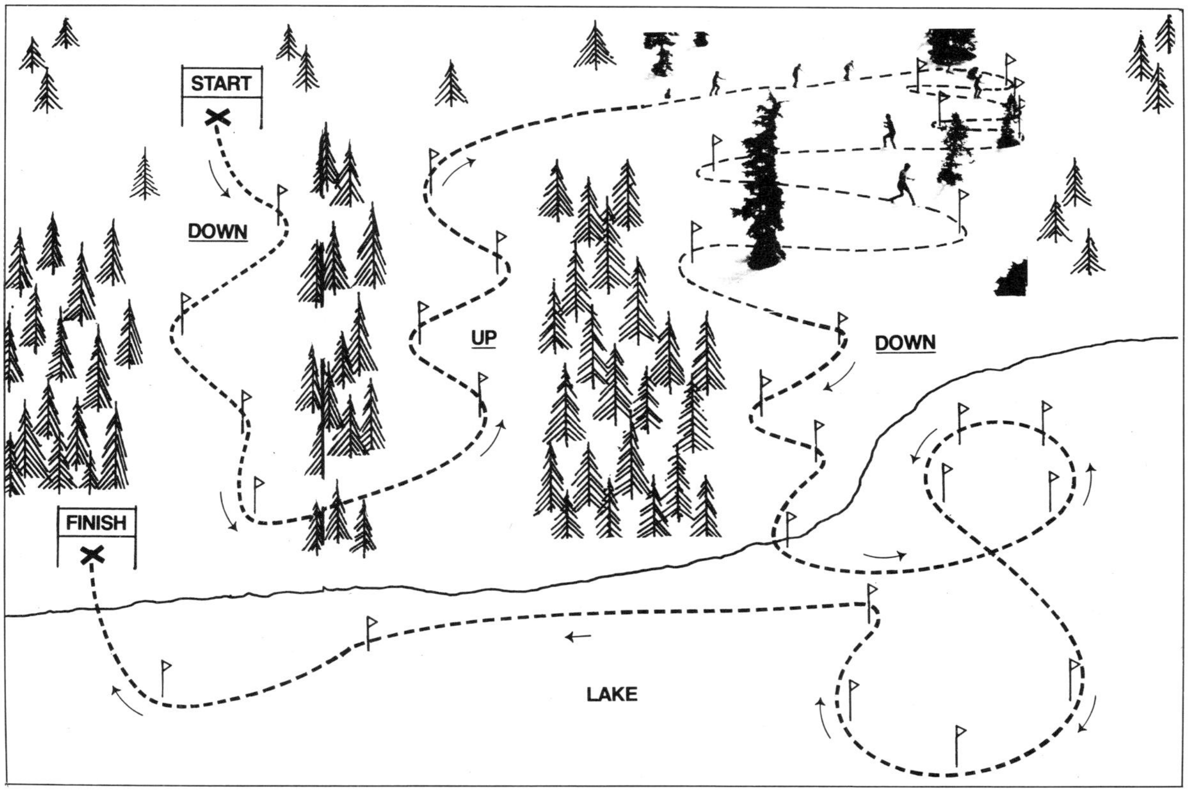
START
DOWN
UP
DOWN
FINISH
LAKE

START
1
3
TIMING BY TIMEX
TIMEX
skiathlon
4
2

105

Rules

The TIMEX Skiathlom is divided into one slalom part, one jumping part, and one cross-country part. The competition will be judged by time-keeping, and the intention is that the three parts shall count equally.

SLALOM PART: This part is to be adjusted according to age, and the slope must be broad, quite undulating and well prepared during the entire competition. The distance between the gates should be 12–20 m. and ordinary slalom stakes are to be used. These are to be marked with gate flags, and if parallel runs are to be used, the one run uses red, and the other, blue flags. There should be at least 6–7 m. between the runs if there are more than one. In the Ski Federation's regulations are rules and advice regarding the technical requirements for the hill and the number of gates. As in ordinary alpine competitions, gate-watches are necessary, and as in the American Berzerkebeinerrennet, there are no demands as to style and technique. If the gate is passed on the wrong side, you are not disqualified, but your time is added to, or you have a penalty round in the cross-country section.

JUMPING PART/JUMPING HILL: In this section it is age and level of skill which is decisive for the lengths. They can be from 2 m. to 15–20 m. for the best. The landing slope is divided into different zones according to the age groups, and if the jump is too short, a penalty round or additional time is allotted. A bonus can also be given for the longest jump. There are to be two or three jumps in the jumping part. There are to be good tracks in all the in-runs, and the jump is to be so low that a low flight results. Here the profile of the hill must be built in such a way that the skier glides at a low height over the hump but at the same time gets a good length. In larger competitons, there should be two or three hills next to each other to avoid queues at the jumping hill. If this is the case, the hills should be placed at least 8 m. away from each other. The penalty rounds should be from 20-40 seconds.

CROSS-COUNTRY PART: In the cross-country race there should be varied challenges so that the skiers have to use different skiing techniques.

To the left
Style is not judged in the jumping part of the Timex Skiathlom. Whether one jumps like a crow or in perfect style makes no difference. It is the length which counts.

TELEMARK CUP IN NORWAY AND THE USA

Already in 1981, a warning was issued in American ski magazines: The Telemark revolution has gone too far! (see p. 78). From being a ski technique to obtain increased joy in skiing in varied terrain, the Telemark style went over to be a branch of competition which became more and more like alpine competitions. The boots became more like slalom boots, clothes and equipment were suited for speed, fashion and skiing through gates, – indeed much of the distinctive character was gone.

The warning from Steve Barnett was taken seriously because he held a strong position within what the Americans call «back-country» ski culture. Therefore, cross-country skiing and the Telemark Cup co-exist, and the ski producers make «Telemark skis» both for competitions and cross-country use.

In the USA the Telemark style is «big business» with professional skiers on the payroll of the ski factories. Large sums of money are involved and many critics have claimed that this can cause Telemark skiing to develop away from what was the original intention.

In Norway the Telemark Cup Competition started in the winter of 1984. It came about as a cooperation between the Ski Industry's joint office and Norway's Professional Ski Instructors' Organization, NPS. The first year there was a competition in Trondheim, Oslo and Hemsedal, with the first enthusiasts on the start lists. The year after, the Cup opened in Morgedal, and later there were competitions in many places. In the winter of 1986, many hundreds took part, and Beate Rønning Arnesen and Hans Gunleiksrud won their separate classes. The winners got a free

In Sweden the Telemark revival has been popular longer than here in Norway. Many clubs have taken up the Telemark style, but it has particularly been associated with the alpine centres. In Norway we have also many clubs, among others the active «Bjørgvin Telemarksvingere» in Bergen.

Bjørgvin Telemarksvingere

Anno 1985

SVENSKA

MAD

Telemark Trophy 1986

STOCKHOLM 26 jan

SLALOM I ULLNABACKEN

Som bästa resultat räknas snabbast i två åk.
Även DIFFERENSSLALOM ingår. Herr- o. damklass.
Arr. TÄBY SLALOMKLUBB.

SÄLEN 15 feb

SLALOM: Som bästa resultat räknas snabbast i två åk. Även DIFFERENSSLALOM ingår.
Herr- o. damklass.
Arr. Tandådalens SKICENTER.

ÅRE 14-16 mars

Crosscountry Downhill Cup

14 mars PUCKELPIST: Här får vi visa vad vi kan och inte kan. Vi kör med freestyleregler och domare från Åres freestyleklubb.

15 mars SLALOM: Som bästa resultat räknas snabbast i två åk. Även DIFFERENSSLALOM ingår. Herr- o. damklass.

16 mars ÅREKÖRET: Som en värdig avslutning klättrar vi upp på skuttoppen, därifrån startar vi mot målet som är på Åre torg. En hemlig idealtid skall prickas. Alla startar samtidigt.

28 mars FISCHER TELEMARK CUP
Slalom i tidsenlig klädsel.

Att fightas om!

Trofén som visar
ALFRED E. NEUMAN
MAD's STÄNDIGE BESKYDDARE

1885 · 1985 SVENSKA TURISTFÖRENINGEN

FISCHER alpina skiboots

TELEVERKET I NYA SPÅR

ANMÄLAN

Åre Sportservice, Kabinbanans dalstation. Tel. 0647/507 40 eller 506 28.
Startavgifter: 150:— för Crosscountry Downhill Cup. 65:— för Telemark Cup.
Anmälan till Stockholmstävlingen sker till Täby Slalomklubb,
Box 3018, 183 03 Täby. Startavgift 65:—.
Anmälan till Sälentävlingen sker till Tandådalens Skicenter,
Box 60, 780 67 Sälen. Startavgift 65:—.
Avgiften betalas i samband med anmälan, då du också får ett utförligt program.
— ALLA SORTER och TYPER av SKIDÅKARE VÄLKOMNA —

SPORT SERVICE Åre

The new Telemark trend has definite opponents among «classic» skiers who attach importance to our correct skiing saga. The new Telemark style has not sufficient roots in the Norwegian skiing saga, but is a branch of American salesmanship in their opinion. The picture on pages 92 and 93 show skiing enthusiasts with different kinds of equipment on the ski trails. However, those who have seen Norwegian young people skiing happily down the hills with Telemark equipment, have a quite different opinion. Increased enjoyment in varied terrain is the object, and the technique is so demanding that a great deal of training is necessary to achieve this goal. The Timex Skiathlom was met with much of the same scepticism, but that is the way it has always been in our ski saga. Future development up to the turn of the century will show whether terrain skiing in its new «Telemark form» will survive.

trip to the North American Championships at Steamboat Springs in Colorado, USA, and in the competition there both skiers came right up to the finals and placed very well.

There are classes for both new and seasoned skiers, and that which distinguishes these competitions from the usual slalom and giant slalom meets, is that the gates are to be passed in correct Telemark style.

In a couple of years, more ski clubs have gone in for Telemark skiing. Svingen Ski Club was among the pioneers and they have in particular kept to Geilo and the hills around Oslo. The city of Bergen and the country of Vestfold are hardly the best known of our skiing areas, but nevertheless they have now their own Telemark clubs. BJØRGVIN TELEMARKSVINGERE has now over a 100 members and the interest in cross-country skiing in the Telemark style is definitely on the increase in western Norway.

In Sweden they took up the Telemark trend from the USA several years before we did. There was considerable talk there about making separate federations for the Telemark enthusiasts. The milieu around the skicentre Åre was particularly active. They have also a Telemark Cup every year, but interest has stabilized in recent years. In Norway we are just at the beginning of something which will spread more and more in the 1990's.

WE HAVE COME A FULL CIRCLE, THE LOOP IS COMPLETED

The picture of Norwegians with knapsack, knitted cap and colourful heavy sweater skiing toward the woods, has become a caricature of the typical Norwegian. When the Holmenkollen railway transports people up in the woods and hills around Oslo, and Easter tourists follow the snow to the highest mountain peaks, this has to do with the distinctive character of our ski culture.

The dangers involved in this ski-touring, have been counteracted by mountain regulations and rescue services, and we have our own rules for sensible clothing in the mountains.

This ski culture has also its pioneers. Fridtjof Nansen, Karl Roll, and in the Alps, Arnold Lunn. It has not been popular to mention in Norway what foreigners have contributed to ski history, but Sir Arnold Lunn has done more to spread mountain skiing in other countries than anyone else. With great emphasis on skiing technique from Morgedal, he wrote, up to the twenties, seven or eight books on this subject. He took up all possible features of skiing and had such a comprehensive outlook that he both laid down the basis for competition rules in slalom, and wrote the book «Alpine Skiing at all Heights and Seasons». Here he wrote about different types of snow avalanches, turning technique, clothes for the mountains and everything which could make the trip easier. The book came out in 1921, and can be a good guide even today.

After the World Championships in Falun in 1974, chemistry became more prominent in the production of skis. Many clung to wooden skis for all-around use, others swore by narrow, glass-fiber cross-country skis with Rottefella bindings also in the mountains. For footwear in the mountains, some people went from solid boots to thin cross-country shoes of fine leather. How many ruined their enjoyment of skiing by using this equipment in the mountains, we shall never know, but it is a fact that several thousand injured themselves and some lost their lives. This is well-known to everyone who has worked with the rescue teams. Equipment which was made for prepared, flood-lit

To the right
Already in the 1880's, city people went to the mountains during winter holidays, while people in the mountain settlements in Telemark went into the mountains to hunt or to visit communities on the other side. Mountain skiing is a part of our national character. Many follow the last patches of snow on ski trips far into May and June.

A SKI TRIP

«George came tearing down in a Telemark position, knees crouched, but with one leg forward and bent and the other dragging behind. His poles hung behind him like a pair of thin insect legs, and whirled up small clouds of snow when they touched the snow on the ground. And finally, this half-kneeling figure with the trailing poles made a beautiful right turn, crouched over, got the skis in the right position – one forward, the other back, while the body provided the right counterbalance for the turn, and the poles indicated the curve as two luminous points - all in a whirl of snow.

«I didn't dare try a Christie,» George said. «The snow was too deep. But you made it beautifully.»

«I can't make a Telemark with this leg of mine,» said Nick.»

(From the short story «Ski Trip» by Ernest Hemingway)

trails and for competitons, was partly dangerous and at any rate totally unsuitable for use in icy, uneven mountain terrain.

On the other hand there were those who claimed that the broad wooden skis which resembled those used by Sondre Norheim, were the best for use in the mountains and uplands, in loose snow or on uneven mountain slopes. This is in many ways true, but also far from practical for most average skiers. The broad wooden skis are too heavy.

Also, for ordinary cross-country skiing the Telemark renaissance has afforded greater skiing enjoyment. The new cross-country skis with Norwegian spruce in the middle, American space technology products all around and steel-edges, opened up a new world for the skiers. The inward curve and tension make turns easier, and the steel-edges grip well on icy slopes. Sturdy Telemark boots can be used in the new solid Rottefella bindings, and these boots are soft to wear and yet firm enough in the turns.

To the left
When one makes a correct Telemark turn, one feels it and rejoices in doing it perfectly. The best way to learn the technique is to join a skiing course or to take lessons at a ski school.

Above right
If you want more drama than you can find in the rounded Telemark mountains, go to the Sunnmøre Alps. Here Øyvind Fet has captured a heavenly day among the Regndal peaks in Sykkylven.

Below right
The new Telemark terrain skis are ideal in the mountains. The steel edges grip well, the skis are light and the boots are stable in all kinds of conditions. The new solid toe harnesses hold the boots just as firmly in the harnesses as when one uses a wire-harness.

It was said about Sondre Norheim that he could do two loops, one after the other. A loop is a turn on skis which continues in a circle until you have crossed your own tracks. According to hearsay, Sondre Norheim managed to do this two or three times! Now he has done it again. The style of skiing that he helped to release in the Morgedal hills over a hundred years ago, is back as the best and most engaging form for cross-country skiing.

In the course of the last 120 years we have developed in many fields. Think of the technical development from 1860 to today! Compared with other means of transportation, none have changed so little as skis. In 10–15 years we have adjusted to the new skis which were introduced in Falun in 1974. We have got cross-country skis that can be used both in the mountains and for touring, with edges that make it possible for us to enjoy a slalom run with the Rottefella bindings. Most of the old tradition is retained, and new technology is more than previously adapted to classic skiing.

The Telemark combination is back with the TIMEX Skiathlom and the development in recent years goes more and more in the direction of MORE FUN ON ONE PAIR OF SKIS! As in Morgedal in the 1860's, Telemark skiing has made a new loop.

A trip in the Norwegian mountains with perfect snow conditions. It is a little cold, but the February sun begins to give warmth. Plenty of food and equipment in the rucksack and sleigh and a good, loyal travelleing companion. This side of modern skiing has developed from the first trips of Fridtjof Nansen, and his journey on skis across Greenland has opened up a completely new experience of winter in the mountains or in glacier terrain.

SOURCES AND LITERATURE

AMUNDSEN, K. VILH.: Skiløpning (Aschehoug, Kristiania 1924)

BARNETT, STEVE: Cross-country downhill (3. edition) (Pacific Search Press, Washington 1983)

BERGSLAND, EINAR: Norsk skiløpning idag (Universitetsforlaget, Oslo 1985)

BJAALAND-MUSEET: Ski og Sudpol (Morgedal 1970)

BØ, OLAV: Norsk skitradisjon (Det Norske Samlaget, Oslo 1966)

ENGLISH, BRAD: Total Telemarking (Crested Butte 1984)

ERIKSEN, STEIN: Mine hvite eventyr (Cappelen, Oslo 1952)

ERIKSEN, STEIN: Come ski with me (W. W. Norton & Co., New York 1966)

FLEMMEN, ASBJØRN: Telemarksvingen (Universitetsforlaget, Oslo 1985)

FORENINGEN TIL SKIIDRETTENS FREMME: Jubileumsskrift 1933

HUITFELDT, FRITZ: Skiløbning i text og billeder (Jacob Dybwad, Kristiania 1908)

KVIGNE ROSTAD, BARBARA (red.): The Saga of Ski for Light (Sons of Norway Found 1985)

LOUPEDALEN, TORJUS: Morgedal, Skisportens vogge (H. Aschehoug, Oslo 1947)

LUNN, ARNOLD: Alpine skiing at all heights and seasons (Methuen & Co, Ltd., London 1921)

NANSEN, FRIDTJOF: Nansens røst (Oslo 1942)

RUUD, SIGMUND: Skispor krysser verden (H. Aschehoug, Oslo 1938)

RUUD, SIGMUND & BIRGER: Sporene videre (H. Aschehoug, Oslo 1945)

SKI, JAN. 1986 COLLECTORS EDITION: (Special Commemorative 50th Anniversary Issue)

VAAGE, JACOB: Norske ski erobrer verden (Gyldendal, Oslo 1952)

VAAGE, JACOB: Skiens verden (Hjemmenes Forlag, 1979)

For further references, see the yearbooks of the Ski Federation and the Ski Association.

ARTICLES

BALDWIN, EDWARD R.: Deep Powder (Nordic Skiing, March 1977)

BARNETT, STEVE: It's gone too far (Cross Country, Oct. 1981)

BURROWS, ART: A Racing Renaissance (POWDER, February 1985)

GULBRANDSEN, STEIN: Telemarksvingen (Skistar 85/86)

HANSON, WAYNE: Cross Country Downhill (Cross Country Skier, Nov. 1981)

HEDLUND, ÅKE: Telemark – Skidkonst och Träkonst (Åka skidor, nr. 2/81)

MEYERS, CHARLES: Telemarking! (Cross Country, Oct. 1981)

PARKER; PAUL: Telemark with an early Lead Change (Cross Country Skier, Dec. 1984)

PARKER, PAUL: Linking turns (Cross Country Skier, Nov. 1981)

RAGG, DAGFINN: Telemarksvingen er tilbake (Snø og Ski nr. 1, 1985)

SHELTON, PETER: Natural Techniques (Outside, Dec. 1984)

TEJADO-FLORES, LITO: Telemarking hits the backcountry (Backpacker Nov. 1982)

WEINSTOCK, JOHN: Sondre Norheim: Folk Hero to Immigrant (Norwegian-American Studies Vol. 29, The Norwegian-American Historian Association, Northfield, Minnesota, 1983)

SKI-SONG FROM SELJORD
The local poet Jørund Telnes lived from 1845 to 1892, and wrote this song about the joy of skiing and the fun on the hills.

When Norway sparkels in her coat of silver,
We put skis on our feet.
Up from the valley we throng in crowds,
And the boys gather on the mountain side.
Where it counts to be hard,
Where it counts to be strong,
Where it counts to be sons of our fathers.

Though icicles form on our shirts,
Our cheeks have a red-hot glow:
We ski down from the cliffs and the peaks,
Enwrapped in a cloud of snow.
Then we jump in the air
And our skis and our bodies
Fly up so it blows at the top.

PHOTOGRAPHS

Associated Press Photo: p. 79
Berg, Karin: p. 14, 40
Dysthe, Bjørner: p. 98
Gastuna Badgastein: p. 56
Fet, Øyvind: p. 97 (top)
Hart, Kim: p. 49 (bottom), 97 (bottom)
Hickey, Patrick: p. 42
Kleppen, Halvor: p. 26, 48, 49, 53, 57, 59, 69 (bottom), 77 (top), 81, 93, 96
Lynau, Jan Petter: p. 30 (top)
Lønborg: p. 6
Mittet: p. 18 (bottom)
NTB: p. 60
Røstad, P. A.: p. 43
Skandinavisk Høyfjellsutstyr: p. 47, 77 (bottom)
Skistar: p. 44
Strand, Haldor: p. 11, 85, 88, 92
Thorkelsen, Th.: p. 55
Trägårdh, S.: p. 95
Vestly, Johan: p. 17, 23, end paper
Vårdal, Sigvald: p. 41
Watson, Bill: p. 65
Wilse: p. 10, 18 (top), 33, 54, 56

Photographs reproduced with the permission of the following institutions (photographer's name unknown):
Pers Hotell, Gol: p. 27, 39 (top)
Skimuseet: p. 16, 21, 25, 30, 33, 35, 36, 51, 54, 63, 66, 71, 74, 79
Åsnes Skifabrikk A/S: p. 39 (bottom)